Jake Gave Her A Look That Defied Interpretation.

Placing baby, cradle and all on the coffee table, he turned to where she stood surrounded by an assortment of baby gear, plus her usual clutter.

Sasha forgot to breathe. Was it only her imagination that made her feel as if every cell in her body turned his way, like a sunflower following the sun?

All it took was the slightest encouragement and she was off on another fantasy, inventing a happy ending that wasn't going to happen.

Jake placed his hands on her shoulders and pulled her into his arms. With her face against his hard, warm chest, she inhaled the scent that was pure Jake Smith.

"Fair warning. I'm about to kiss you," he said calmly.

"Go ahead," she said in a voice only an octave or so higher than normal. "I dare you."

Dear Reader,

Welcome to another scintillating month of passionate reads. Silhouette Desire has a fabulous lineup of books, beginning with *Society-Page Seduction* by Maureen Child, the newest title in DYNASTIES: THE ASHTONS. You'll love the surprises this dynamic family has in store for you...and each other. And welcome back *New York Times* bestselling author Joan Hohl, who returns to Desire with the long-awaited *A Man Apart*, the story of Mitch Grainger—a man we guarantee won't be alone for long!

The wonderful Dixie Browning concludes her DIVAS WHO DISH series with the highly provocative *Her Fifth Husband?* (Don't you want to know what happened to grooms one through four?) Cait London is back with another title in her HEARTBREAKERS series, with *Total Package*. The wonderful Anna DePalo gives us an alpha male to die for, in *Under the Tycoon's Protection*. And finally, we're proud to introduce author Juliet Burns as she makes her publishing debut with *High-Stakes Passion*.

Here's hoping you enjoy all that Silhouette Desire has to offer you...this month and all the months to come!

Best,

Melissa Jeglinski

Melissa Jeglinski
Senior Editor
Silhouette Desire

Please address questions and book requests to:
Silhouette Reader Service
U.S.: 3010 Walden Ave., P.O. Box 1325, Buffalo, NY 14269
Canadian: P.O. Box 609, Fort Erie, Ont. L2A 5X3

DIXIE BROWNING

Her Fifth Husband?

🌷 Silhouette® *Desire*

Published by Silhouette Books

America's Publisher of Contemporary Romance

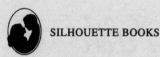 **SILHOUETTE BOOKS**

ISBN 0-373-76641-6

HER *FIFTH* HUSBAND?

This edition published by arrangement with Harlequin Books S.A.

® and TM are trademarks of Harlequin Books S.A., used under license.
Trademarks indicated with ® are registered in the United States Patent
and Trademark Office, the Canadian Trade Marks Office and in other
countries.

Visit Silhouette Books at www.eHarlequin.com

Printed in U.S.A.

Books by Dixie Browning

Silhouette Desire

Shadow of Yesterday #68
Image of Love #91
The Hawk and the Honey #111
Late Rising Moon #121
Stormwatch #169
The Tender Barbarian #188
Matchmaker's Moon #212
A Bird in Hand #234
In the Palm of Her Hand #264
A Winter Woman #324
There Once Was a Lover #337
Fate Takes a Holiday #403
Along Came Jones #427
Thin Ice #474
Beginner's Luck #517
Ships in the Night #541
Twice in a Blue Moon #588
Just Say Yes #637
Not a Marrying Man #678
Gus and the Nice Lady #691
Best Man for the Job #720
Hazards of the Heart #780
Kane's Way #801
*Keegan's Hunt #820
*Lucy and the Stone #853
*Two Hearts, Slightly Used #890
†Alex and the Angel #949
†The Beauty, the Beast and the Baby #985
The Baby Notion #1011
†Stryker's Wife #1033
Look What the Stork Brought #1111
‡The Passionate G-Man #1141
‡A Knight in Rusty Armor #1195
Texas Millionaire #1232
The Bride-in-Law #1251
§A Bride for Jackson Powers #1273
§The Virgin and the Vengeful Groom #1331
More To Love #1372
Rocky and the Senator's Daughter #1399
The Millionaire's Pregnant Bride #1420
**Beckett's Cinderella #1453
**Beckett's Convenient Bride #1484
Social Graces #1550
Driven to Distraction #1568
††Her Passionate Plan B #1628
††Her Man Upstairs #1634
††Her Fifth Husband? #1641

Silhouette Special Edition

Finders Keepers #50
Reach Out To Cherish #110
Just Deserts #181
Time and Tide #205
By Any Other Name #228
The Security Man #314
Belonging #414

Silhouette Romance

Unreasonable Summer #12
Tumbled Wall #38
Chance Tomorrow #53
Wren of Paradise #73
East of Today #93
Winter Blossom #113
Renegade Player #142
Island on the Hill #164
Logic of the Heart #172
Loving Rescue #191
A Secret Valentine #203
Practical Dreamer #221
Visible Heart #275
Journey to Quiet Waters #292
The Love Thing #305
First Things Last #323
Something for Herself #381
Reluctant Dreamer #460
A Matter of Timing #527
The Homing Instinct #747
Cinderella's Midnight Kiss #1450

Silhouette Books

Undertow 2003

Home for the Holidays
"Christmas Eve Reunion"

Lone Star Country Club
The Quiet Seduction

Silhouette Christmas Stories 1987
"Henry the Ninth"

Spring Fancy 1994
"Grace and the Law"

World's Most Eligible Bachelors
‡His Business, Her Baby

**Outer Banks
†Tall, Dark and Handsome
‡The Lawless Heirs
§The Passionate Powers
**Beckett's Fortune
††Divas Who Dish*

DIXIE BROWNING

has won numerous awards for both her paintings and her romances. A former newspaper columnist, she has written more than one hundred category romances. Browning is a native of North Carolina's Outer Banks, an area that continues to provide endless inspiration.

One

Stealing a few moments from the job, Sasha lay back on the chaise longue, closed her eyes against the late-afternoon sun and savored the warm sea breeze that fluttered her georgette camisole. She might not have a regular salary, much less benefits, but this beat a desk in a cramped, windowless cubicle all to pieces.

The sound of distant traffic merged with the nearby sound of the surf to become a soothing lullaby. "Five minutes," she murmured.

Five minutes and then she would jump up, finish checking off her list, think of anything she might have forgotten and then stop by another client's new office complex to see how long before she could get started there.

As an interior designer, her bread and butter consisted of professional suites—usually law, real estate or medical. Occasionally she did between-season patch jobs for rentals in the various beach communities along the northern Outer Banks, but her real love was having a brand new McMansion to do from scratch. Any budgetary limits only stimulated her creativity.

She sighed in contentment. When the soft southeast breeze blew her hair across her face, she smoothed it back, still without opening her eyes. If she had the energy she would take off her shoes, but that would require sitting up and bending over to unfasten the ankle straps. She should have worn mules.

"Vanity, thy name is Sasha," she murmured. The trouble with pointy-toed, stiletto-heeled shoes was that they were so darned flattering she couldn't *not* wear them, even knowing she'd be climbing up and down all these wretched stairs.

She actually owned a few pairs of flats, though she seldom wore them. At home she went barefoot and wore shapeless tents, but anytime she went out in public she took pains to look her best in case she ran into a potential client. Her friends, knowing her background, called it the Cinderella syndrome.

Sasha had never denied it. Underneath the careful makeup, the streaky cinnamon-tea hair and the fashionable outfits bought at end-of-the-year sales—not to mention the jewelry she adored—Sasha Combs Cassidy Boone Lasiter was still plain old Sally June Parrish, oldest daughter of a dirt-poor tobacco farmer turned preacher.

At times like this, she almost wished she didn't give a damn. She wondered if Cinderella's feet had hurt in those miserable-looking glass slippers.

"Relax, feet," she murmured drowsily. "Once we get home you can let it all hang out, I promise."

The sun felt marvelous now that it had lost most of its midday heat. A natural redhead—sort of—Sasha freckled whether or not she wore foundation with a serious SPF.

One more minute, she promised herself. After that she would go back inside and finish her check-off list. The cleaning crew had come and gone last week, but the place still reeked of cigarette smoke. Not only that but one of the bedspreads was rumpled, as if whoever had made it up had been interrupted before they could finish the job. King-size beds probably required a team to do the job right.

Housekeeping, however, was not her responsibility. She had listed the items that needed replacing. Chair cushions, flatware and a few dishes that had probably been taken out on the beach and lost, one chair with a broken leg, a stained lampshade and two leather-topped bar stools that looked as if they'd been used as targets in a game of darts. Normally the owners would have handled it, but according to Katie McIver, who managed several cottages in the area, the owner of Driftwinds had called at the last minute and asked her to find someone else to bring the cottage up to standard for the upcoming season.

Sasha had worked with Katie before. This was a peanuts job, but small jobs lead to larger ones and she was in no position to turn down any commission, no matter how small. In the case of the Jamison cottage, if the owners wanted their investment to pay off, Katie or someone needed to screen their clientele, if that was legally possible. The last tenants had waxed surfboards in one of the showers, leaving an unholy mess for the poor cleaning crew.

Sasha massaged her temples, taking care not to involve her long, acrylic nails. The headache that had been threatening all day was getting closer to a reality. She'd counted on a few minutes of complete relaxation to take care of it, but so far it wasn't working.

One more minute, she promised herself. After that she would go back inside and finish making the rounds. She'd already noticed what looked like a red-wine stain on one of the bedspreads that the cleaners had missed. People who had everything—people who could afford to rent one of these million-dollar-plus rentals—too often valued nothing.

Think peaceful thoughts, she willed silently. Think of bittersweet chocolate melting on your tongue. Alan Jackson singing softly in your ear. Nordstrom's and a no-limit charge card.

Here she was in a beachfront cottage—if a six-bedroom, seven-bath house complete with two hot tubs and a swimming pool could be called a cottage—and her blasted sinuses refused to allow her to enjoy it.

She was still attempting to talk herself into relaxing before her headache got any worse when a shadow passed over her. Without opening her eyes, she frowned. A shadow of what? According to Katie, this entire row of cottages was empty until Memorial Day weekend.

Opening her eyes, she blinked against the late-afternoon sun. There wasn't a cloud in the sky, not even a vapor trail. Yet even with her eyes closed, she could've sworn a shadow had just passed over her.

Probably a pelican, she thought, and relaxed again. Sasha hadn't grown up in this part of the state, but she did know that long before the developers had taken possession, these dunes had belonged to sea birds, sand fiddlers, a few hardy fishing families and a herd of wild ponies.

Sighing, she let her eyes drift shut again, conscious now of the reddish-brown color of sunlight seen through mauve-shadowed eyelids. She was almost asleep when it happened again. Reddish-brown briefly turned dull black and then back again. Warily, she opened her eyes, lifted her head and looked around.

Nothing moved. Not even a mosquito.

More curious than afraid, she tried an experiment, closing her eyes, she passed a hand over her face, just to be sure.

There it was again—that momentary darkening. Something had definitely blocked the sun for one split second. A fast-moving airplane? Flight-seeing tours were common in the area, but usually not until the season got underway. Besides, unless it was a glider, she would have heard it.

She struggled to sit up, because whatever it was, it wasn't her imagination. There was simply nothing up there to cast a shadow. No birds, no planes—not even a flying superhero. Whatever it was that had passed between her and the sun was gone.

And dammit, so was any chance of relaxing.

She was still struggling to get up off the low chaise longue when she heard a soft thump and what sounded like a muffled exclamation. Pulses pounding, she glanced over her shoulder. Sunlight reflected off the sliding-glass doors behind her, blocking her view of the interior. Logic told her that no one inside could have cast a shadow over the outer deck, but logic was the first victim when a woman was truly spooked.

Had she locked the lower door when she'd let herself in? With her mind on so many things at once, details occasionally escaped her attention. Katie could have seen her car and dropped by to check on her progress. Maybe one of the cleaning crew had left something behind. Or maybe they hadn't finished, which would explain the stained bedspread and the cigarette smell.

But that still wouldn't explain a shadow crossing over the upper deck.

Gripping the sides of the low chaise, Sasha called out, "Dammit, who's there?" Bracing her feet, she readied herself to dash inside and lock the sliding doors. "Listen, whoever you are, I'm tired, my feet hurt and I've got a killer headache. You don't want to mess with me!"

Okay, so she'd been reading a lot of thrillers lately—crime was a sad fact of life, even here in an oceanfront paradise. Like most of the upscale cottages, Driftwinds had a state-of-the art security system.

Which she hadn't bothered to re-arm….

Well, shoot. She had the instructions written down somewhere—what numbers to punch in and how long to wait and what to do next. But she hadn't planned on being here long today, so it simply hadn't seemed worth the effort.

Uneasiness gave way to alarm. Oh, God—what if she had to run for it? She wasn't exactly one of the kick-ass heroines that were so popular now. As much as she abhorred exercise, she had to admit there were times when physical fitness came in handy.

Crossing to the nearby wooden rail, she peered down at the paved parking below. The only car there was her own red convertible.

So it wasn't Katie, and it wasn't one of the cleaning crew. Warily, she glanced over her shoulder toward the outside stairs, half expecting to see someone step out onto the upper deck. The lack of logic didn't bother her—she'd figure out later how someone downstairs could cast a shadow upstairs.

What was it everyone said? Get real?

Real fact number one: a work crew armed with pneumatic hammers had invaded her skull.

Real fact number two: she'd just finished her period, so her hormones were probably involved, too. Which didn't help matters.

Real fact number three: she had probably imagined the whole thing.

Sighing heavily—again—she turned to go inside. That's when she saw the figure silhouetted against the sunset on the upper deck of the cottage next door. The cottage that was supposed to be empty.

They stared at each other across the fifty or so feet of beach sand that separated the two elaborate cottages. He was holding something in his hand—something that was aimed directly at her.

A *gun?*

She swallowed hard and forgot to breathe. It was impossible to tell what it was from this distance. The only gun she'd ever met up close and personal was the old .410 her father used to use for squirrel- and rabbit-hunting.

The thing she was staring at now was small and squarish. Actually, it looked more like some kind of a camera than a gun, but then, there were all sorts of weird weapons in use these days. Tapers—tasters—something like that.

Common sense—admittedly not her greatest strength—said that if he'd meant her any harm, he would have made his move when she'd been lying there half-asleep and helpless. He was probably just taking pictures for one of the rental agencies. She would never even have noticed him if his shadow hadn't passed over her.

Against the low-angled sun, she couldn't make out his features, but his silhouette indicated broad shoulders that tapered to narrow hips before his body disappeared behind the deck railing. Before she could clamp down on it, her imagination supplied a few more details, and she turned away in disgust.

"It has to be these flaming hormones," she muttered. For all she knew he could be an escaped prisoner who'd spent the winter hiding out in a closed cottage, which was a whole lot more comfortable than hiding out in the mountains like Eric whatsisname, that guy who had eluded the FBI for about a dozen years. Only now that the season was about to get underway, he had to get out and find another hiding place. As for those shoulders, he'd probably developed them busting rocks on a chain gang. Maybe that thing he was holding was one of those gizmos that broke glass or read the combination on a wall safe, or—

She simply *had* to stop reading so much romantic suspense!

What was that old saying about the better part of valor? In the stress of the moment it escaped her, but right now the better part of valor was slipping inside where she'd left her purse and dialing 911 on her cell phone, just in case. Like any sensible woman, which she devoutly hoped she was, but secretly suspected she wasn't, Sasha had the emergency number on speed dial.

Pretending nonchalance, she crossed to the sliding doors, slipped inside and looked around frantically for her purse, breathlessly watching over her shoulder for someone to burst through the door.

"Hello? Yes, this is Sasha Lasiter. I'm at Driftwinds cottage in Kitty Hawk." She gave the milepost and the street number—at least she remembered that much. "Look, there's a man in the cottage next door that's supposed to be closed, and either he's pointing a weapon or taking pictures of me. Yes, I'm sure!" she replied indignantly when asked. "Well, whatever that thing is he's holding, he was aiming it at me."

Maybe he was—maybe he wasn't, but if she wanted help she needed to make out a worst-case scenario. "Look, I know—" She broke off in exasperation. "No, I am *not* in the hot tub! I am fully dressed, but I *happened* to be outside on the upper deck, and—" Impatiently, she explained what she was doing in an unoccupied cottage. "I don't *remember* if I locked up behind me or not!" She was pretty sure she hadn't. She listened as the flat voice gave instructions, then broke in and said, "Look, I am not about to take a chance on reaching my car and risk being mugged, so could you please send someone to check him out?"

Feeling discouraged, a little bit frightened and in no mood to finish what she'd started earlier, she refused to stay on the line. Instead, she headed for the kitchen and located a block of kitchen knives. Armed with a filet knife that she would never have the nerve to use, she made her way back upstairs and looked around for the most defensible place to wait. She hadn't been lying when she'd told the dispatcher she was afraid to go outside. A friend of hers had recently been mugged in a parking lot not two miles from here. Her own car was parked close enough to the house so that she could probably unlock it with a remote, jump in and lock it again before anyone could grab her, only her remote didn't work anymore—she wasn't even sure it was still in her purse.

Besides, how safe was a convertible? The top was aluminum, not rag, but even if she got away, who was to say the creep wouldn't follow her home?

Who would ever have thought that being an interior decorator at a beach resort could be a hazardous occupation?

"Hey, Jake. We just got a call from some lady that says you're spooking her out." The lanky deputy stepped onto the upper deck from the outside stairway.

"Hey, Mac. How'd you know it was me?"

"Call came from next door, but I saw your wheels parked outside, figured you'd know what was going down. You working?"

"I was. Sorry if I upset the lady. I yelled at her, but she'd already gone inside."

"Oh, yeah—like yelling at a woman always sweetens 'em up. So, you want to tell me what you're doing? She said you were either aiming a gun at her or taking her picture."

"Pictures. Hell, Mac, you know I can't tell you who I'm working for." John Smith, otherwise known as Jake, squinted against the low-angled sun. "Divorce case. Woman thinks her husband's got a little something going on the side. She wants some backup evidence before she files. I figured I'd check out their cottage first since it was empty. The guy's pretty well known in the area, so I figured he wouldn't risk being seen at a motel with another woman."

"Any luck?"

"Not yet. I just started today."

The deputy nodded. Mac Scarborough had been three years ahead of Jake's son, Tim, at Manteo High, but they'd known each other the way people in small towns did. Then, too, being in the security business, Jake knew most of the lawmen in the surrounding area.

"How's Timmy? He gone over there yet?" the young deputy asked.

"Shipping out any day now." Jake shook his head. "I don't mind telling you, I wish he'd joined you guys instead of the army."

"Yeah, well...wait a few weeks till the season cranks up. You'll be glad he's over there working on heavy equipment in a war zone instead of rounding up DUIs and busting up drug deals and trying to untangle pile-ups at every intersection between Oregon Inlet and the Currituck Bridge." The deputy shook his head. "Ah, hell, man, I'm sorry."

Jake ignored both the reminder of his loss and the apology. "You wouldn't trade your job for one any place else in the world, and you know it."

Grinning, the younger man removed his hat and raked his fingers through short, sun-bleached hair. "You got that right. I guess nothing goes on here on the Banks that don't go on a whole lot more in the big cities. Leastwise, here we get to go surfing on our day off." He replaced his hat, angling the brim just so. "Reckon I'd better go next door and let that poor lady know you're one of the good guys."

Knowing that whatever chance he'd had of collecting evidence was shot for the time being, Jake said, "Might as well, now that you've scared my red-feathered pigeon off."

"Hey, at least I didn't use my lights and siren." Mac grinned and turned toward the outside stairway. "You take care now, Jake. Tell Timmy I said hey and don't go upsetting any more ladies, y' hear?"

Just then they heard a door slam. Mac hesitated, and then both men leaned over the rail in time to see the shapely redhead run that awkward way women did when they were wearing those ridiculous shoes. She unlocked the door to a fancy red convertible and climbed in, her miniskirt-covered hips being the last thing to disappear before she slammed the door, backed out of the driveway and scratched off down the beach road.

"Well, hell," the deputy muttered.

"Guess that takes care of that," Jake said.

He'd just have to try again tomorrow. Waste another day, probably. Common sense told him if anything was going on over there, as his client seemed to think, it would be during the day, not at night when lights might arouse curiosity in a supposedly empty cottage. The day wasn't a total loss, though. The redheaded woman had obviously been waiting for someone.

He packed away his digital camera, shoved his sunglasses back on his face and jogged down the outside stairs, his mind on the comely redhead. Except for the hair, she reminded him of that classic poster of Marilyn Monroe, especially the ankles. A little shorter—maybe a little rounder. Whoever she was, she had what it took to tempt any man between the ages of can-do and can't-do.

On the other hand, he mused as he climbed into his middle-aged, slightly rusty SUV, since she'd called the law, there was some room for doubt as to her identity. Would she have done that if she'd just stopped by for a little afternoon delight with Jamison?

Either way, pictures of the woman alone weren't going to do Mrs. J. any good. He must've snapped off a dozen shots from different angles before she'd wakened up and caught him at it.

At age forty-one, Jake Smith, owner of a small security business, had allowed his PI license to go largely unused while he was single-handedly raising his son. A few years ago he'd taken a refresher course at Blackwater, one of the world's best security training outfits, which happened to be just up the road in the next county. But as there was far less demand for private investigators than there was for security engineers, he'd concentrated on the latter. Even so, as a spook, even a slightly rusty one, he knew enough to take down the license number of any potential suspect.

Which he had—and which he should have asked Mac to run for him. They occasionally traded favors, JBS Securities and the sheriff's department.

She'd cut over to the bypass and headed north. So did Jake, even though it was getting late and he lived in the opposite direction. On the way, he placed a call to his second-in-command. "Hack, I need some information quick. Red Lexus convertible, I make it about an oh-two model, vanity plate S-A-S-H-A."

"Gimme a minute." The nineteen-year old electronics whiz snapped his gum and ended the call.

Hack was as good as his word. By the time Jake

reached the point of decision—whether to take a right and head toward Southern Shores and points north, or turn west, cross the Wright Memorial Bridge over Currituck Sound and go from there, he had an address.

Muddy Landing. Slapping his hand against the steering wheel, Jake didn't even try to come up with a logical reason for what he was doing. There was a good barbecue place on the way, and he hadn't taken time for lunch.

As for what he hoped to accomplish, that was another matter. The sexy little redhead might or might not have been waiting to meet Jamison, who might or might not have been delayed, scared off or otherwise held up. In an area where either of them might have been recognized, it stood to reason they wouldn't risk meeting in a more public place, not when Jamison owned a big empty cottage with all the comforts of home.

On the other hand, the woman could have had legitimate business there. She might be a rental agent, or even a potential renter. Before he dumped the pictures he needed to find out whether or not she was involved. She was definitely tempting enough, especially compared to Jamison's wife.

But no matter how great the temptation, carrying on an affair in a property you owned was pretty stupid.

He passed the barbecue place, inhaled deeply and promised himself to stop in on his way back. More an overgrown community than a town, Muddy Landing was small enough so that he had little trouble locating the address, even without the gizmo Hack had installed in the SUV.

Nice place, he thought as he pulled up two houses down on the other side of the street, although he wouldn't have chosen to paint a house light purple—orchid or lavender, whatever the color was called—with dark green trim and a red car parked in the driveway. But what the hell, no one had ever accused him of having good taste.

Jake considered the best way to approach her. "You looked like a hot number, so I decided to follow you home," probably wasn't going to cut it. She'd slam the door and call the cops, same as she'd done before, and this time he couldn't blame her.

On the way up the front walk, he tucked in his shirttail and ran a hand over his thick, dark hair. While he waited for someone to answer the doorbell, he took in the details of the well-kept two-story house. He liked the fact that not all the houses were the same style or color. From here he could see three whites, two yellows and a blue. When it came to color, the influence of the nearby beach had evidently spread inland. Over on the Banks, the county commissioners had actually considered limiting the colors a property owner could use. Talk about government running wild. At least on his own two properties in Manteo, some 40 odd miles south, he stuck to plain white, inside and out. Nobody could complain about that. He was in the process of having the duplex repainted and the roof re-shingled, partly because of storm damage, but mostly on account of it was long overdue.

He pressed the button again and was about to give it another try when the door opened. "Ma'am, my name's Jake Smith and I—"

He got no further than that when a short creature with raccoon eyes growled at him. "Leave me alone, I don't want any, I'm not interested, and I don't do surveys."

"Oh, hey—" Jake had the presence of mind to wedge his foot in the opening before she could slam the door shut. "I'm not—that is, I've got credentials." When he reached for his wallet, she lunged and stomped on his foot. Pain streaked all the way up to his groin. "Legitimate business," he grunted through the pain. Quickly, he flashed his PI license and the sheriff's courtesy card he'd been given years ago, that had no official bearing, but hell, he'd have shown her his mama's recipe for cornmeal dumplings if he thought it would help.

"Ma'am, I just wanted to apologize—to explain in case you were still worried."

Was this even the same woman? Same height, same hair color, but instead of that hot little number she'd been wearing less than an hour ago—red miniskirt, thin flouncy top and a pair of sexy spike-heeled ankle-strap shoes—she was covered from the neck down with what looked like a deflated army tent. Her feet were bare, with red toenails and red places on the sides where those pointy-toed shoes had rubbed. As fetching as they were, shoes like that were a crime against nature.

He lifted his gaze to her face while his own throbbing foot held the door open. When a hint of some exotic fragrance drifted past, he inhaled it, eyes narrowing in appreciation.

"You're dead meat," she said flatly. "There's a deputy living two doors away. All I have to do is call him."

"You want to use my cell phone?" He made a motion as if to get it, although he'd left it in the truck.

She blinked and relaxed her death grip on the door. At least, her fingers were no longer white-tipped. Actually, they were red-tipped to match her toenails. "Just state your business and leave," she said grimly. "I'll give you thirty seconds and then I'm calling Darrell."

He might have taken her more seriously if she didn't have eye-makeup smeared halfway down her cheeks. At least he hoped that's what the black and blue stains were, otherwise this might be a worst-case domestic situation. The hair that reminded him of the color of heartwood cedar was mashed flat on one side, standing up on the other. His wife used to call it bed-head.

Hell, maybe this was where she was meeting Jamison. Could they have got their signals crossed? That perfume she was wearing smelled like torrid sex in a tropical garden.

But then, why would she be dressed like this to meet a lover?

Not that even dressed in what looked like a Halloween costume gone wrong, she wouldn't make any normal man think of tangled sheets and damp, silky skin.

"Would you please remove your foot?" she demanded.

Khaki-colored eyes. He could've sworn they were some shade of blue, but then, at any distance of more than a dozen feet, eye color was hard to discern. "Ms. Lasiter, I just wanted to reassure you that—"

The black-rimmed, khaki-colored eyes widened. "How did you know my name?"

Jake thought, I'm too old for this. No matter how good she looked under that disguise—no matter how good she smelled, it just wasn't worth the wear and tear.

But she deserved an answer, and he'd come here expressly for that purpose. Among other things. "I'm in the security business and I was on a job I had to check out your license I'm sorry if I upset you I just wanted you to know you're in no danger from me." He said it all in a single gust of breath, hoping she wouldn't finish breaking every bone in his foot. Now he knew how a fox felt when it was caught in a steel trap.

Jake Smith, Sasha thought. A variation of John Smith. Right. How likely was that? Staring through bleary eyes, she tried to convince herself that the man who called himself Jake Smith was on the level. Silhouetted against the sunset he'd been impressive enough. Up close and personal, he was—

Yes, well regardless of what he was, she didn't need any. Didn't need it, didn't want it, knew better than even to think about it. By the time she'd got home her headache had grown to the four-alarm stage, which meant pills alone weren't going to do much good. Nevertheless, she'd downed three with a swallow of milk from the carton. Then, not bothering to remove her makeup, she'd shed her clothes, pulled on her oldest, most comfortable caftan and fallen into bed with a package of frozen peas over her eyes.

"Just so you know," he said, "I'll probably be there again. I'm not finished with my job."

Even in her semi-demented state, she couldn't help but notice that he was sort of attractive, his tanned, irregular features bracketed by laugh lines and squint lines. Under a shadow of beard there was a shallow cleft on his square jaw. A few strands of gray in his dark hair. Obviously he'd reached the age where a man either started to fall apart or ripened into something truly special.

This one was ripe.

"Well, just so you know, neither am I," she warned,

belatedly coming to her senses. "Finished with my business, that is."

He stepped back, freeing his foot. She didn't wait for him to turn away before slamming the door.

Two

Distracted enough without trying to drive and eat at the same time, Jake ordered a barbecue plate to go and drove the rest of the way to Manteo, a distance of some forty miles, listening to a Molasses Creek CD and thinking about the unusual woman he'd just met.

Sasha Lasiter. It had a ring to it. He wondered if it was her real name. The first thing he'd noticed about her back at the Jamison cottage was her shape. That thing she'd been wearing when he'd tracked her down might have covered her curves, but he'd already seen 'em first-hand. The short skirt and that wispy thing she'd been wearing on top, while it was a lot more than most women wore at the beach, barely covered the essentials. His imagination had filled in the rest.

A guy didn't see curves like that every day. Jake had heard about hourglass figures. Hers fit the description, with maybe twenty-minutes more sand in the bottom than in the top. The fact that those same generous curves extended all the way down to her ankles meant it was probably genetic and not silicon.

Damned fine genes, he mused.

The scent of barbecue drifted up to his nostrils as he crossed the Washington Baum Bridge over Roanoke Sound and headed home. He had a feeling that it might take more than 'cue and fries to satisfy him tonight. His sex life had died of neglect while he was single-handedly raising his son.

Almost as tall as he was, Jake's wife Rosemary had been a local track star and dreamed of making the Olympic team. They'd gone to school together, K through twelve. In the tenth grade Jake had made up his mind to marry her. They'd eloped the week they'd graduated—by that time she had given up on her Olympic dreams. Neither of them had ever regretted it.

Seven years later Rosemary had been killed by a drunk driver at one of those intersections Mac had mentioned. Because of their son, Timmy, Jake had managed to hold it together—just barely. After a year or so of fighting the memories, he had rented out the house he and his wife had bought cheap, decorated on a shoestring and shared, and moved himself and his son into the other side of the duplex where his office was located.

God, how long ago had it been? Sometimes he had trouble visualizing her face. Looking at the pictures—which he hadn't done lately—no longer seemed to help. Not that the styles back then had been all that different—blue jeans were blue jeans; shorts were shorts. But the goofy, self-conscious grins on their faces, especially after Timmy had been born seven-and-a-half months after they'd been married, were hard to relate to after all these years. There were pictures of the tree house he'd built when Timmy was six months old and of the rust bucket they'd bought as a second car and been so proud of.

Somewhere over the next dozen or so years, his memories had turned to memories of photographs instead of memories of the real thing.

"You're getting old, man," he muttered as he let himself into the empty duplex, dodging around a folded drop cloth and two ladders. Funny thing, though—he didn't feel old. As tired as he was and as much as his right foot was starting to ache, he felt younger than he had in years.

Sasha woke when early sunlight slanted through the window across her pillow. Without opening her eyes she lay there for several minutes, thinking of yesterday and the color of light and shadow seen through closed eyes. Holding her breath, she waited to see if her headache was going to smite her again.

The word *smite* reminded her of her father, who had frequently smote with his fists, even after he'd gotten religion. It also reminded her that the church-sponsored box suppers would soon be starting up again, which steered her thoughts directly to the matchmaking game she and her friends had played for the past several years. Daisy had married and moved to Oklahoma. Marty had married, too, but still lived on Sugar Lane. Faylene, the maid they shared, was an invaluable member of the matchmakers, and the weekly box suppers were one of their favorite venues for getting two people together.

They still hadn't found anyone for Lily, the CPA who had moved to Muddy Landing a few years ago. The yachtsman they'd tried last fall hadn't worked out. He'd sailed away; she'd stayed put. Faylene, who cleaned for Lily, had mentioned the letters she got weekly from somewhere in California, that she always put away in a bedroom drawer instead of her desk.

Not that that meant anything, especially as Faye said the letters were written in pencil on lined paper. So maybe she had a child by a previous marriage. Or maybe a niece or nephew...

One who wrote once a week?

Sasha thought of her own nieces and nephews. She was lucky to see their signatures on the birthday and Christmas cards her sisters sent.

Rolling over onto her side, she thought about Jake Smith, wondering if he was married or otherwise involved. If not, they might want to add him to their list of candidates. Whatever else he was, he was definitely one studly hunk.

As random thoughts came and went—she was always at her most creative early in the morning—she made a mental note to check with Katie at Southern Dunes Property Management to see if there were any new cottages going up. Might as well get her bid in early.

Satisfied that her headache was gone, her sinuses no longer in rebellion, she sat up, did a few minimal exercises and headed for the shower.

Jake Smith had said he wasn't finished with whatever it was he'd been doing in the cottage next door. Adjusting the water temperature, she wondered idly what he'd been doing when the deputy she'd called had showed up. She'd seen the two of them together just before she'd made a run for it. Whatever it was, he hadn't been arrested, so it was probably nothing illegal, after all.

My mercy, that felt good! Hot water beat down on her shoulders, softening the muscles where stress always grabbed her. She could do with a good deep-tissue massage if she could ever find time.

He'd said he was in the security business. He'd probably been either installing a new system or repairing an old one, in which case he was probably one of those technical types who spoke a language she'd never even tried to master. She used a computer only because she had to, but she wouldn't know a RAM from a nanny goat, a gig from a crab-net. She read instructions only when she was forced to and even then she rarely understood a word. When it came to disarming and re-arming the gizmos people used to protect their property, she usually managed to follow simple written instructions of the do-this-and-then-do-that variety, but occasionally she screwed up and had to call for help. Basically she was a big-picture woman in a small-picture world.

So he was a security man. Big deal. He and Lily would probably find loads of things in common to talk about in intricate detail.

Increasingly relaxed, Sasha worked coconut-scented, color-care shampoo through her thick, wavy hair. She was still toying with questions and answers concerning yesterday's mini-adventure when she dried off, lotioned generously and dressed for work in a long skirt topped with a yellow T and a gauzy camisole. Her skirts were getting just a wee bit snug in the hips. Not in the waistbands—whenever she gained a pound, it went straight to her hips, never her waist or her boobs. If she'd been born a century earlier she'd have been right in style, complete with a built-in bustle.

Unfortunately, long, lean and selectively silicon-enhanced was today's style. As she was none of the above, she was forced to make the best of what she had.

Which she did with—she hoped—style, taste and panache.

By the time she had breakfasted on a doughnut—just one, as she was dieting—and a homemade latte and gotten dressed, the temperature had climbed into the low seventies. As there wasn't a single cloud in the sky, she put down the top on the convertible that had been her thirty-fifth birthday gift to herself. Her foundation was a high SPF, but even so she tied on a wide-brimmed hat, letting the scarf-ends trail out behind her.

Hadn't some famous actress died that way when her scarf got tangled around a wheel? She might not have a college degree, but she prided herself on having a wealth of trivia at her fingertips.

Just past the bridge over the Currituck Sound, she stopped at her favorite coffee shop and ordered a hammerhead to go. In case her headache threatened again—and even if it didn't—she could do with the double shot of caffeine.

Several minutes later she pulled into the paved parking area beside the Jamison cottage. A single glance told her that the parking area next door was empty. She refused to admit to being disappointed. Judging from what she knew about men—and she could have written a book on the species—the studly security man was probably still in bed.

A morning person herself, Sasha had practically been forced to pry all four of her ex-husbands out of bed. Frank had been born lazy. Barry had worked nights, which gave him a legitimate reason, she admitted reluctantly. But Rusty had simply preferred to sleep late and play late, gambling and partying till all hours, usually without her.

As for Larry, her first husband, met and married in a mad, mad weekend the month before she'd turned nineteen, she couldn't even remember what his excuse had been, unless it was because he knew it drove her crazy. Even as a child she'd been up with the sun, bursting with energy.

The truth was that not a single man she'd made the mistake of marrying had possessed anything resembling a work ethic. Even her father, redheaded, stern-faced Addler Parrish, had sold his tobacco farm and taken up preaching.

Not that he was very good at that, either. Everyone said old Ad was mean as a snake, and she could personally vouch for that. But at least the hours suited him better, giving him plenty of time to lay down the law to his family and punish anyone who broke his rules. Which Sasha had consistently done.

She'd been plain Sally June Parrish back then. Her overworked mother had lacked the strength to defend either herself or her children from her husband's vicious tongue, much less from his belt and his fists. As soon as Sally June could escape she'd left home and found a job stocking and clerking in a furniture dealer's showroom. Within a few years, she began taking night classes at the community college and attending the International Furniture Market in High Point with her employer.

By that time she'd been married to Larry Combs, a Jude Law lookalike who couldn't manage to hang on to a job for more than a few months. He'd claimed to be overqualified. What he'd been was under-motivated. Larry had been the first. Her second husband had been even better-looking, and witty, besides.

Unfortunately, he'd also been a crook.

With two brief marriages behind her, she had left the Greensboro area and started her eastward migration, eventually leaving behind two more ex-husbands. None of her marriages had provided her with what she so desperately needed—a close and loving family. And none had lasted much longer than a year. By the time she'd moved to Muddy Landing and set herself up as an interior decorator, Sally June had become Sasha. She had stuck with her fourth husband's name because it was easier than changing everything again.

Besides, it sounded good with Sasha.

She'd chosen Muddy Landing because at the time, property in Currituck County had been comparatively cheap. That was rapidly changing as more and more of it was developed, but the location was perfect, being little more than an hour from the Norfolk shopping area and less than half that from the Outer Banks where building was booming and decorating jobs were plentiful.

That had been eleven—no, nearly thirteen years ago. Once it gathered momentum, time seemed to fly. At the age of thirty-eight, thirty-five years of which she admitted to, Sasha was single for keeps. Each time she'd married she'd been certain she'd finally found her prince.

Instead she'd found another poor jerk who thought that learning to dress and speak well would alter who he was. Underneath the designer sportswear, the fancy colognes and the rip-off Rolexes, they'd all been every bit as insecure as she had once been, the difference being that they'd lacked her guts, her brutal self-honesty and her relentless drive to succeed.

She might joke with her friends about looking for number five, but before she would ever allow herself to get involved with another man, she would let her hair go natural, dump all her makeup in the North Landing River and turn her jewelry into fishing lures.

Parked in the shade of the Jamison cottage, she sat outside for a few minutes, savoring the perfect spring weather and the last of the double-strength coffee. She should be able to wind things up here in an hour, with some time to spare.

Opening the door, she swung her legs out and sat there for a moment, savoring the relative quiet of the early morning. A week from now, traffic would have doubled and most of the cottages would be filled, but for now the quiet cul-de-sac was almost like a private retreat.

Leaving the top down, she trudged up the first flight of outside stairs, unlocked the main door and disarmed the security system. The place still smelled of stale cigarette smoke, so she left the sliding glass doors open to air it out. Mosquitoes weren't yet a problem as they'd had a record dry spring. On the next level up, she opened another door, drawing air from below.

At least she didn't turn the air-conditioning full blast with all the doors and windows open the way too many thoughtless tenants did.

Humming under her breath, she began double-checking the list she'd made yesterday to make sure that everything that had been lost, stolen or damaged had been replaced. The new bar stools had been delivered. She checked that off her list. Climbing to the top level, she took a good look around to confirm that she hadn't overlooked anything. Once she was done, she slid open the glass doors on the top floor and stepped out onto the sundeck, her favorite place of all. Ignoring the spectacular view of dunes and ocean, she glanced at the cottage next door.

Not that she'd expected to see him—the parking area next door was empty. Not that she even wanted to see him, but he'd said he wasn't finished with whatever it was he was doing over there—installing, updating or repairing a security system.

She told herself she wasn't disappointed, and really, she wasn't. Not for herself. But for months now she and her friends had been looking for a candidate for Lily Sullivan, the beautiful blond CPA with the sad eyes who lived a few streets over from Marty's house. So far as anyone knew—Faylene could find out more about a person from their garbage alone than any CIA agent— Lily had no social life at all.

The trouble was that there were so few available men around—certainly none who might interest a woman who was both attractive and intelligent. The best had already been taken; the rest were too old, too young, too dull or too dumb.

Ironically, over the past couple of years it had been Daisy and Marty, two of the original matchmakers, who had skimmed the cream off the top, with Daisy marry-ing Kell Magee when he'd come east to check out a relative, and Marty marrying the yummy carpenter she'd hired to renovate her house.

And she wasn't envious, she really wasn't! As she turned to go, one of her heels slipped between two boards. Flailing her arms for balance, she grabbed at the chaise longue, which slid away from her, throwing her even more off balance. Pain shot up her left leg. Trying to catch herself as she went down on her behind, she jammed her fingers on the sun-warped deck.

"Oh, help, oh, shoot, oh, damn, damn, *damn!*" She rocked back and forth, clutching her ankle with one hand and waving the other hand in the air, her shoe heel still trapped in the crack between boards.

Seeing that the pink suede covering the five-inch heel was ruined, she cried out in frustration as well as pain. She'd paid dearly for these shoes, knowing that nothing flattered a woman's legs like a good pair of spike heels. Especially a woman who had stopped growing—at least vertically—in the fifth grade. Having been told at an early age that redheads shouldn't wear pink, she'd gone out of her way to wear something pink on every possible occasion, even if it was only pink tourmaline jewelry.

With trembling fingers, she managed to unbuckle the ankle strap, unwrap it and ease her foot from the arrow-shaped toe that looked so gorgeous she usually didn't even notice the torture.

Oh, gross! Her ankle was already starting to look like an overstuffed sausage. Not only that, she had popped three fingernails and collected a handful of splinters that would probably give her blood poisoning. Didn't they use arsenic to treat the lumber for these beach houses? Did that include the sundecks?

At least she managed to unfasten her gold ankle bracelet before it cut off circulation. Oh God, she was going to die right here on the top deck of an empty cottage. The sun would turn her red as a boiled crab. Her nose would blister, seagulls and ospreys would drop disgusting things on her body—

Her cell phone—she'd left it in her purse inside. If she could just get up she could use one of the plastic chairs as a walker and hop inside to call 911. Although after yesterday...

Maybe a different dispatcher would be on in the mornings.

Tears streamed down her cheeks, leaking trails of mascara through her blusher, dripping off her chin onto her Tilly MacIntire blouse. She unfastened her other shoe and tossed it aside. What good was one shoe when its mate was ruined? If it weren't for the fact that nothing flattered a woman's legs like putting them on a pedestal—and she was just vain enough to want every advantage she could possibly get—she'd burn the treacherous things the minute she got home.

But first she had to get there.

She was on her knees, trying to grab the leg of a chair and drag it closer when she heard someone step out onto the sundeck behind her.

"What the devil have you done to yourself?" a familiar voice boomed.

Startled, she twisted around and stared up at the voyeur—the man who had scared the wits out of her just yesterday.

Oh, please, her inner woman groaned, not like this!

"Help?" she said weakly.

* * *

By the time they were in Jake's SUV on the way to the hospital in Nags Head, Sasha had set aside her misery to make three firm vows. First, no more five-inch heels—at least not when she was working. Second, starting now she would cut her carb count in half. No more Krispy Kremes, no more double lattes.

In other words, no more anything worth eating.

Jake had insisted on carrying her down the stairs. As her only option was bouncing on her butt all the way down, which would've left her rear end in the same shape as her right hand, she'd let him sweep her up into his arms. As if pain alone weren't bad enough, the feel of being cradled against a hard, warm body had rattled her to the point that she hadn't even argued.

She'd already forgotten the third vow, but it probably concerned steering clear of any man who could melt her resistance with no more than a growl, a glower and the way he smelled. Like soap, toothpaste and coffee, plus something earthy and essentially male.

Not to mention the fact that his touch alone was like poking her finger into a light socket.

She'd still been quivering inside when he'd settled her onto the passenger seat and arranged something to prop her foot on. He'd reached for the seatbelt and she'd brushed his hands away. "I can do it myself."

"Then do it," he'd snapped.

What the devil did *he* have to be angry about, she wondered, feeling sorry for herself and, oddly excited at the same time. She was the one with a broken ankle, not him. She was the one whose right hand was probably going to get infected and swell up and have to be amputated. Plus, she'd probably end up with blood poisoning. For all she knew she might be allergic to antibiotics. So she'd die of anaphylactic shock or whatever grisly symptoms that sort of allergy caused.

He drove fast, easing off each time he approached the stoplights so that he wouldn't have to slam on the brakes if a light suddenly changed. Grudgingly, she appreciated it. Her ankle throbbed like a bad toothache, and she hated pain, purely hated it. Always had. A stoic, she was not.

"You all right?" he asked as they passed the Wright Brothers Memorial at Kill Devil Hill. At least he'd quit growling. In fact, he sounded almost concerned.

"No, I'm not all right, I hurt," she snapped. Childish, but then, what did she have to lose that she hadn't already lost? Her dignity?

Ha.

"We'll be there in a few more minutes," he said. "This time of year, you probably won't have to wait. They'll give you something for pain and then do X-rays, my guess." He had propped her foot up on a plastic carton he'd padded with a folded shirt. She was cradling her splintery hand in her other hand on her lap. "What's wrong, did you hurt your hand, too?" he asked.

Well, shoot. Now he even sounded sympathetic. She couldn't handle sympathy. It had been in short supply back when she could have used it—back when she'd spent her lunch money on cheap makeup to conceal bruises inflicted by her father's fists, only to have him accuse her of painting her face like a hussy. Which often as not earned her a few more bruises.

Jake pulled up in front of the beach hospital and said, "Wait while I go get a wheelchair."

"Don't be silly, I don't need a wheelchair." She had never even been to a hospital before, except as a visitor.

"Okay then, put your arm over my shoulder." He leaned into the open door and eased his arm under her knees.

If she'd had a single rational thought in her head before, it was gone by the time he carried her inside. The man was definitely high-voltage.

"You'll have to do the paper work," he told her, "but I'll see if I can't speed up the process."

Two women behind glass windows stared. Several people in the waiting room glanced up from their outdated *People* magazines.

"Oh, for heaven's sake, put me down," Sasha muttered. At this rate she wouldn't even need a doctor's help. Being this close to Jake Smith, whoever he was—whatever he was—was distracting enough that she hardly even noticed her throbbing ankle, much less her stinging hand.

Just under two hours later an orderly wheeled her out to the waiting room. Laying aside the newspaper he'd read without retaining a single word, Jake stood to meet her. "All done?" he asked. No cast, just a wrap job, which meant a bad sprain, not a break. "What's with the hand?" Her right hand was bandaged, all but two fingers and her thumb.

"Splinters. I lost three fingernails, too."

His eyes widened. "Good God, that's awful!" he swallowed hard, fighting back nausea.

"I think another one's loose and I just had them done last week. Now I'll have to get the whole right hand done over." Glancing over her shoulder, she thanked the orderly. "I can make it from here just fine," she assured him with a smile that was undiminished by chewed-off lipstick and smeared mascara.

"It's the rules, ma'am," the orderly said, refusing to dump her out of the wheelchair.

Jake shook his head. He crossed to the double glass doors and held it wide. "Come on, don't be so stubborn."

Together, the two men eased her from the wheelchair onto the front seat. Jake slipped the orderly a few bucks—didn't know if it was proper or not, but the kid was about Timmy's age. Might even have been a classmate.

They drove several miles in silence except for a few heavy sighs coming from the passenger side. The first time they stopped for a red light, Jake tried to get a handle on how bad she was hurting. "We'll stop by and get your prescription filled, then we'll cut over to the beach road and put the top up on your car. It should be all right there for a few days until you can drive."

"Oh, wait a minute—just hold on, I'm not leaving my car unattended."

"You feel up to driving?" He looked pointedly at her ankle, which was once again propped on the padded carton.

"It's not a stick shift."

"Sasha—Ms. Lasiter—look at it from my perspective. If I dump you out in Kitty Hawk, I won't sleep a wink wondering if you made it home all right. It'd be criminal negligence at the very least if anything happened to you." They must've given her something for pain. From the way she was blinking her eyes, the lady was floating around in la-la land.

"I can call a taxi."

"That won't help you move your car. Look, I got you safely to the hospital, didn't I? Don't you trust me to get you home?"

Another milepost zipped past. He turned off onto the street that dead-ended at a row of oceanfront cottages that were identical but for color and the placement of a few exterior details. Driftwinds, where she'd left her car, was the next to last one on the cul-de-sac.

"You shouldn't have to drive me all the way to Muddy Landing."

She was softening, he could tell. Truth was, he didn't know why he was going to all this trouble. He should be working on the Jamison case, especially since so far his stakeout had produced zilch.

"You like barbecue?" he asked, climbing back into the SUV after pulling her car into the paved space underneath the cottage, putting the top up and locking it.

Nice wheels. The lady had good taste. He handed her the keys and backed out onto the street.

"Who doesn't?" She was picking at the bandage on her hand, and he reached over and covered both of hers with one of his.

"Leave it alone," he said. "Didn't your mama ever tell you not to pick at stuff like that?"

That warranted a fleeting smile. He had a feeling she was hurting more than she wanted to let on, even after whatever they'd given her at the hospital. Which was kind of surprising, because judging by her looks alone he'd have figured her for a complainer.

Not until some ten minutes later when he came out with two barbecue plates and climbed back under the wheel did it occur to Jake that either they were going to share a late lunch or he was going to eat his share cold somewhere else. "Should I have gotten some drinks to go with it?" he asked as they rolled onto the bridge over Currituck Sound.

"I've got iced tea," she said, which pretty much answered the question.

"Tea's good." Jake pushed in a CD and whistled under his breath, keeping time with the music with his thumb tapping against the steering wheel.

With work piling up, his home and his office in a mess and the Jamison case going nowhere, he had no business being where he was, doing what he was doing. He'd never been the impulsive type.

On the other hand, when he started something, he always liked to carry it through. In his business, following procedure was the only way to get the job done.

Oh, yeah? And what have you started this time?

Three

Sasha desperately needed to reach her own front door unaided, if only to assert her independence, but after the first few steps she grudgingly accepted Jake's help. This had definitely not been one of her better days. Awkwardly, she dug out her keys. He took them from her uninjured hand. "It's the key with the fingernail polish," she told him.

Independence could wait another few minutes.

Without releasing her, he managed to unlock the front door. "Want me to carry you over the threshold?"

Her look said it all. Over my dead body. Sprained, splintered and disheveled didn't count.

Once inside, he steered her toward the three-cushion sofa. "First, let's get you elevated. Then if you'll point me to the kitchen, I'll make you an ice pack."

"How do you know what I need?"

This time it was *his* look that said it all. "Trust me, I've seen a sprain or two. Underneath that bandage you're probably already turning purple."

Sasha wanted to tell him to take his sympathy and his barbecue plate and go back to wherever he came from, because she didn't need him.

Only she did. This was Faylene's day to work for Lily, and Marty was just back from her honeymoon, still busy washing sand and salt out of her trousseau.

"The doctor called it a type-II sprain. He said something about torn ligaments, but I wasn't really listening." Admittedly, she had a few bad habits, one of them being deflecting bad news by concentrating on something else. In this case, she'd been focused on the possibility of insuring her more expensive shoes. "He mentioned ice. I think there's a gel pack somewhere in the freezer, but I usually use frozen vegetables."

"You do this often?"

While she gave him her patented supercilious look—naturally arched eyebrows tinted half a shade darker than her hair helped—he eased her down onto the sofa and gently lifted her legs up onto the cushions, which involved a lot more touching than she needed at the moment. Her skirt twisted around her hips and she tugged at it with her good hand, wishing she'd worn something longer. She had mini and maxi, nothing in between.

"Here, let's lift your foot up and slide a pillow under your heel." His voice was like blackstrap molasses—rich and sweet, but with a definite bite.

While she wondered where he came by his expertise, he slipped another pillow under her knee, which involved more touching. Considering she was still in appreciable pain, even after a dose of prescription-strength anti-inflammatory medication, she shouldn't even have noticed. If she didn't know better, she might think her whole body had been sensitized. The slightest brush with sumac and she broke out in a rash. The slightest brush of Jake Smith's hands on her thigh or the back of her knee raised goose bumps in places he hadn't even touched.

Granted, she'd been on a self-imposed diet these past few years, but she wasn't *that* starved for masculine attention.

He stepped back and looked her over. "There, that better?"

Wordlessly, she nodded, feeling her cheeks burn. The curse of a redhead's thin skin. "This is so embarrassing."

"No need to be embarrassed, it could happen to anybody."

If she read him right—and she was good at reading people—he might as well have added, Anybody crazy enough to wear skyscraper shoes lashed to her ankles. Was there such a thing as breakaway ankle straps?

"How's the hand?" His were on his hips. Tanned, capable hands planted firmly on narrow masculine hips.

Just quit thinking what you're thinking! "It's fine." She looked down at the fingers she'd jammed. Her newly exposed natural nails looked like naked little orphans.

"Sit tight, I'll be back with your ice pack in a minute."

"No hurry. I think I'll get up and tap dance on the coffee table."

He shot her a quick grin as he headed for the kitchen. Distracted, she almost forgot her misery. He had a nice smile. He had a *really* nice backside, which she noticed only because it was more or less at her eye level as he left the room. Strong legs, too—at least he hadn't dropped her when he was carrying her down all those steps.

Not that she would have fallen too far, the way she'd clung to him with both arms.

"Peas or corn, either one will do fine," she called after him.

"Got it."

"You do this a lot?" he asked again a few moments later as he shaped a bag of frozen peas around her bandaged ankle. "Use ice packs, I mean."

"Headaches," she said, and then snapped her mouth shut. Just because he happened to be there when she'd needed a hand—just because he'd driven her to the hospital and waited for her, stopped at the drive-in window of the pharmacy while her prescription was being filled, taken care of her car for her and then driven her home after stopping to get barbecue—that didn't mean he needed to know her entire life history.

On the other hand, there was Lily, who definitely needed a man if Faylene could be believed. This one just might fill the bill if he happened to be available. The fact that he wasn't wearing a wedding ring didn't mean he was single. Some men didn't.

"Won't your wife be worried?" Well, that was really subtle, wasn't it?

"I called the office to say I might be late."

Was that a yes or a no? Even if he was single, he might not be right for Lily. Men who stayed single past their midthirties were usually confirmed bachelors. She'd read that somewhere.

On the other hand, Muddy Landing's primo match-makers never actually forced a couple to the altar. They simply engineered meetings between needy people in a setting that ensured they'd have to spend a little time together. Not all relationships had to end in marriage. The truth was, marriage itself ended many a good relationship, as both Sasha and Marty could confirm. Between them they'd gone through six husbands, Marty's current bridegroom not included.

"Nice pictures," Jake said, glancing around the cluttered living room.

The rest of her house was even worse. Her personal art collection, which could best be called eclectic, hung in a haphazard pattern on the lime-washed cedar paneling—haphazard because whenever she added to it, she was forced to shift things to make room. Stacked on the floor were nine framed reproductions for two offices she was presently doing.

"Food and a cold drink coming up," Jake said.

In the kitchen, humming under his breath, Jake took a moment to get his bearings. The lady sure did like color. Nothing matched except for a couple of the appliances. One red wall, a couple of pink ones. No curtains at the window, but a bunch of vines hanging down both sides that looked more like sweet potatoes than flowers. But then, he was no gardener—that had been Rosemary's department.

He filled two tumblers with ice, covered the ice with tea from a pitcher in the refrigerator and looked around for a serving tray.

Two o'clock on a workday—not that every day

wasn't a workday—and he was goofing off as if he had all the time in the world. The last time he'd had lunch with a lady was—

Hell, he couldn't even remember the last time.

"Here we go, two barbecue plates, two iced teas," he said, sounding like a snake-oil salesman as he walked into the living room. "You want your barbecue reheated?"

"No thanks, it's fine this way."

"Me, too. Reheating always does something to the flavor."

His social skills had grown rusty with disuse. Small talk defeated him. Besides, what could a hot babe who lived in a lavender house and drove a red Lexus convertible possibly have in common with a middle-aged widower who lived in a half-furnished white-on-white duplex—one who drove a six-year-old SUV with a primer-coated fender he'd never gotten around to repainting?

He watched as she reached for a hush puppy with her good hand. "Why don't I bring a towel to spread over your lap? Eating sideways is kind of awkward."

What was awkward was his being here. He should have just brought her home and left her. Although if he'd done that, she might have gone without lunch. Supper, too.

Ah, hell, she had plenty of friends she could've called on for help. With her looks she probably had to beat off men with a stick. "Look, I can eat in the kitchen if you'd rather be alone. Or leave and take mine with me."

"Oh, for Pete's sake, pull up a chair and use the coffee table. Move the rest of that stuff onto the floor."

He slid her magazines, books and mail to one side to clear a space on the table and drew up a cane-bottomed chair that had two monkeys carved on one of the back panels. She had unique tastes, he'd say that for her. Colorful, too. The rug was one of those oriental types, mostly orange and black. As for the pictures on the wall…yeah, *unique* just about covered it.

"It's an Eisher," she said, following his gaze. "The one beside the escritoire."

As he didn't know an escritoire from an estuary, Jake only nodded. "Interesting," he said, which was usually a safe comment. "You want catsup for those fries?" That was even safer.

Condiments at hand, they applied themselves to the late lunch. It was getting on toward three. Oddly enough, the silence wasn't all that uncomfortable. At least it wouldn't have been if he could have stopped watching her trying to manage with one injured hand and the other one handicapped by long, red fingernails and several rings.

He'd have offered to feed her, but he didn't trust himself to get that close. As it was, it might take a while before he could forget the way she'd felt in his arms when he'd carried her down the outside stairs at the cottage, and from there in to the hospital. As small as she was, there was nothing fragile about her. She was firm, but soft where a woman should be soft.

And then there was the way she smelled, like orange blossoms and incense with a few exotic spices tossed in. Under the right circumstances something like that could easily set off a riot.

In other words, look, but don't touch.

So he looked. The suntan stopped a few inches from the bandage on her bum ankle. Did that mean it was one of those spray-on jobs?

Yeah, probably. With legs like hers, she could've painted them blue and it wouldn't have mattered. Her lips were shiny from the fries and the hush puppies and those thick black eyelashes made her eyes look like the color of the surf in August, before the storms got it all churned up.

Hmm, that was odd. He could've sworn they were tan just yesterday.

Oh, man. That perfume must be messing with his head.

He cleared his throat. "If you're finished, I can take your tray. You want your cell phone handy?" Rising, he looked around for her purse.

"Why would I want that?"

"In case it rings so you won't have to get up? Or to call someone to come stay with you?"

"If it's important they'll call back, and I'm not in the mood for company."

"I just meant—" He started to explain and gave up on it. When it came to defenses, the lady could give lessons to a porcupine.

So he took her leavings to the kitchen, refilled the tumbler with ice and sweet tea and brought it back. Then he removed the cold pack, which was mostly melted, anyway. "Wait a little while, then ice up again. In the meantime, keep your foot elevated. I'll put your prescription here where you can reach it. Let's see…you took the last dose about two." He glanced around for a clock. She looked at her wrist. One of her several bracelets turned out to be a wristwatch. "Every four hours or as needed," he reminded her.

Sasha was glad he'd turned away. She hated being seen at a disadvantage, she purely hated it! She must look like a lump of raw dough with her clothes all twisted around her; with her hair falling out of the carefully casual do she'd started out with this morning and her lipstick chewed off. Heaven only knew what had happened to her eye makeup. At least she'd done nothing to smear her eyeliner or dislodge any of her eyelashes.

"You moonlight as a nurse, right?" she snapped, and was immediately ashamed of herself. She refused to apologize, and that bothered her even more, because she knew better.

Without a word he blotted the rings of moisture from the coffee table, then replaced her magazines and sample books. That mouth of his that could look so sensuous in unguarded moments had tightened into a grim line.

Sasha felt lower than dirt, yet she couldn't bring herself to apologize for her rudeness. God, she was wicked! That saying about pride going before a fall had been one of her father's favorite quotations, usually uttered right before he attempted to beat the pride out of her.

Obviously it hadn't worked.

Jake stepped back, his face expressionless. "If you're sure you don't need anything else, I'll be leaving. Don't forget to ice up again."

"Hand me my purse before you go, I haven't paid you for lunch. I owe you gas money, too."

He looked annoyed, but his voice remained calm. "Just make sure you call someone to sit with you. Tell 'em to bring a book so you won't have to entertain them if you'd rather not, but you're in no shape to take care of yourself."

"Oh, go to hell," she shot back. This time she really would have apologized, but before she could find the words, he was gone. Twisting around to look through the front window, she watched him stride down the front walk. Lordamercy, he looked like a storm waiting to happen. Not that she could blame him.

"Why do I do these things?" she moaned, flopping back onto the cushions. Talk about being your own worst enemy.

Jake was halfway across the Currituck Sound when his cell phone sounded reveille. He punched on and before he could say a word Sasha started rattling off what sounded like an apology, with a garbled explanation that he was in no mood to hear. He broke in, reminding her that she would need someone to take her to Kitty Hawk for her car once she was able to drive again.

"Don't you worry about that one bit," she said earnestly, "I have lots of friends."

He assured her he wasn't worried in the least.

So how come, he wondered as he replaced the phone in its holder, he was trying to think of some excuse to turn around and go back to Muddy Landing?

As to that, how the hell had she gotten hold of his number?

"Dammit, Hack, you know better than to give out my number," Jake said some forty-five minutes later as he slammed the door of his office. The whole damn place reeked of paint. No wonder Miss Martha found so many reasons to stay away. He'd have opened all the windows and cut off the air-conditioning, but Hack insisted the ever-present humidity was lethal to computers.

"The Lasiter woman? Hey, she called here and shot

me this line of bull about leaving something in your car. How was I to know she wasn't on the level?"

"You're paid to know, dammit."

"Whoa, I'm paid to put together the stuff you design and then see that it works. Miss Martha's supposed to handle the phone—that's what you hired her for—only she left early today to go to a funeral. Where you been, anyhow? The Jamison woman called a few hours ago, said for you to call her right back. I tried to get you."

Jake expressed himself in a single succinct oath. A few hours ago he'd been on his way to the emergency room. Hack could have reached him easily…except that he'd left his cell phone in the car.

He had already punched in the first three digits of the Jamison woman's number when it hit him. He didn't have a damn thing to report—at least nothing that was going to help her case.

He replaced the phone without completing the call while Hack looked on, his thin face showing equal parts of amusement and curiosity. Without a word, Jake opened the door to his private office, which was roughly the size of three phone booths and was currently crowded with five phone-booths' worth of stuff that had been shifted from room to room as the painting progressed. The entire duplex was undergoing repairs that had been put off too long. The roof had been damaged in last fall's hurricane and a tree had damaged it further when it had fallen on one corner of the house during a hard northeaster. Things were generally in a mess.

And so was he.

Her shoe. When he'd carried her downstairs from the sundeck, he'd scooped it up and stuck it in his hip pocket, then tossed it onto the back seat. No way was she going to get those straps around her ankle anytime soon, but if she wanted the thing, he could drop it off tomorrow. Or the next day. No hurry, he told himself as he reached for the Jamison file.

On the other hand, it wouldn't hurt to call and let her know he had it.

Sasha hobbled to the bedroom and changed into something more comfortable, then took out a bag of corn from the freezer and settled back on the couch to call her friend. Marty and Greg had just returned from honeymooning at a place called Isla Mujeres, otherwise known as the island of women, in the Mexican Caribbean. "Hi, you rested up from all those sleepless nights yet?"

She switched the phone to the other ear and adjusted the cold pack on her ankle. Earlier she'd removed the bandage to see how bad it looked, as if she'd needed the reminder of just how stupid she could be when she put her mind to it. From now on whenever she had any more than three steps to climb, she would wear sensible shoes if it killed her—as it probably would. Anything labeled *sensible* was definitely lethal to the ego.

"Look, I might have somebody for Lily," Sasha said without preamble, and then had to wait through another rapturous description of everything from the Mexican cuisine to the music to the local legends. She'd heard it all yesterday. "About this man for Lily?" she said when her friend paused for breath. "I'm pretty sure he's single. He's about an eleven on a scale of ten, and—"

She listened to a spate of questions and a recipe for

huevos rancheros, Isla-style. When she could squeeze in another word, she said, "Thanks, hon. Compared to Faylene I'm a regular Julia Child, but I'm not about to try to cook anything I can't spell. Now, back to Jake— I don't know if he's currently involved or not, we'll need to check on it, but—"

Sasha tapped her remaining acrylic nails on the coffee table as her thoughts returned to the man who had taken her other shoe and thrown it away, for all she knew. He hadn't called back, but then, she'd been on the phone practically ever since he'd left. First she'd called her friend Daisy to see when the baby was due, then she'd called the hospital to ask how long before she could drive again.

Evidently the hospital wasn't about to invite a lawsuit by offering an opinion without another on-site examination, which wasn't even a faint possibility. She had several hundred dollars more out-of-pocket expense before her high-deductible insurance would kick in. She wasn't even certain how her policy treated emergency-room visits, as she hadn't bothered to read the fine print.

"Who, Daisy?" she repeated as Marty's excited voice recalled her to the present. "She's due in about three weeks, I just talked to her. Greg promised to let me know, and I'll fly out."

"But you hate flying," Marty reminded her.

"My sinuses hate flying. The rest of me can take it or leave it, as long as it's in first class." For Daisy, she would risk a monster headache. The third member of the original matchmaking trio, Daisy was expecting in June, and Sasha had promised to stand as the baby's godmother. A godchild, even one out in Oklahoma, might help fill the sense of emptiness that been growing inside her for years.

It was that same feeling of emptiness, not to mention a ticking biological clock that had driven her through four marriages in search of a prospective father for the child she wanted so desperately. She'd been married to husband number four when she discovered that, thanks to an early bout of endometriosis, her prospects for motherhood were dismal, at best.

"Okay, hon, then I'll see you in a day or so," she promised and laid her cell phone on top of a wallpaper sample book.

The antique monkey chair made an acceptable walker as long as she took care to plant all four legs squarely on the floor. She hadn't mentioned her accident to Marty, knowing her friend would drop everything and rush over. If there was one thing Sasha didn't need, it was hovering friends. She'd been called the proverbial hog on ice more than once, but she prided herself on her independence. It hadn't come easy.

She was halfway to the kitchen to exchange defrosted corn for frozen peas when the phone rang again. She was tempted to ignore it, but she'd been expecting a call from the Driftwinds property manager.

Instead of Katie McIver, she heard a male voice that affected her like velvet sliding over naked skin. "Hi, Cinderella, you missing a slipper?"

Four

"You have my shoe?" she said breathlessly. Sasha was never breathless, not unless she'd just dashed up three flights of stairs. Definitely not over the mere sound of a voice—or even over half a pair of shoes that had cost far more than she could afford. As miserable as they were, the suffering was worth it when it added five extra inches to her height and called attention to her best feature—her legs.

"The heel's pretty messed up," Jake told her, "I guess you could peel off the rest of the leather and paint it to match the other one. Want me to bring it to you?"

"Oh, that's too much trouble." Unconsciously, she smoothed her disheveled hair. She was wearing her comfortable old caftan and hadn't bothered to put on her face.

"I'll be up in your neck of the woods this afternoon."

He paused, as if testing the atmosphere. "I could drop it off then."

She wanted to tell him not to bother, but even more than she wanted her ruined shoe back, she wanted to see him again. Considering the way they'd met—considering even more her deplorable record with men—it didn't make a speck of sense. But there it was. All she had to do was look at Jake Smith to forget everything she'd ever learned about men. He wasn't even all that handsome, technically speaking. But then, fancy looks, fancy clothes, fancy cars and fancy manners weren't worth a lick of spit when push came to shove.

At least nothing about Jake Smith was fancy.

Nothing except for the way he made her feel.

Besides, he'd already seen her at her worst, looking like a raccoon with eye makeup smeared over half her face, wearing an ancient caftan that should have been relegated to the rag bag years ago. And that was even before he'd risked a hernia by carrying her down all those stairs.

Had anyone ever noticed that good Samaritans could be sexy as well as useful?

"I suppose as long as you're coming this way, you might as well drop it off," she said as graciously as possible.

"See you in about an hour, then. You need anything I could pick up for you? I'll be passing by a couple of shopping centers."

Her mind fogged out on her. All she could think of was her hair, her face—the awful thing she was wearing.

"No? Okay, see you later then. If you think of anything you need, call me on my cell phone, all right? You have the number."

He waited. She waited. Neither of them spoke until he said, "Where are you, anyway, lying down?"

"I'm halfway between the living room and the kitchen," she told him as she clumped her way toward the sofa.

"Have you iced up lately? Look, the sooner you quit fooling around, the sooner you'll be able to drive again."

She was tempted to ask if that meant she had a choice between driving or fooling around. Fortunately, common sense intervened, because the choice was not even close.

He's for Lily, you dunce!

Nearly two hours passed before Jake pulled up in front of the lavender house with the dark green trim. He glanced at the rearview mirror and raked a hand through his hair. He was overdue a trim, but at least he was freshly shaved. Restless, he'd woken about five and gone next door to the office, where he'd made inroads in the stack of paperwork on his desk until the roofers had started hammering.

Shortly after that, Hack and Miss Martha had come in and he'd gone next door to shower and shave before the crew arrived to finish painting. A few more days, he thought as he headed north on the bypass, and the old place was going to look pretty damn good, if he did say so himself.

He happened to be wearing the new polo shirt Timmy had given him for his last birthday. Jake had taken it as a hint that his wardrobe could use some attention—at least the kid hadn't given him a necktie. He'd even splashed on a little cologne, God knows why. Keep the stuff from going bad in the bottle, probably. He never used it.

Some forty-five minutes later he reached into the back seat for the paper cone of flowers. They'd been right beside the checkout counter at the grocery store. He'd made a quick stop, figuring Sasha probably needed a few basics—more frozen vegetables, maybe some juice, a six-pack of canned drinks and a box of doughnuts. Milk, too, because bones needed calcium. And flowers because—because, well, why not?

He punched the doorbell and then tried the knob. It turned and the door opened. "Sasha? Don't get up." A security specialist, he thought about mentioning her unlocked door but decided against it. Right now she didn't need to be jumping up every time the doorbell rang.

With two plastic sacks and the six-pack in one hand, the flowers in the other, he peered into the living room. "There you are," he said, stating the obvious.

And there she was, looking even better than he'd remembered.

Jake had never been partial to redheads—he'd never been partial to any particular type, for that matter. Rosemary had been tall, lean, blond and athletic. But the way Sasha looked with her hair all soft and coppery around her face and her eyes shining like emeralds—

Emeralds? Yesterday they'd been blue.

The day before that they'd been tan.

"Those are lovely," she said, her full red lips widening in a smile.

Jake stared at the bouquet he was holding as if he'd never seen the thing before. "Uh—yeah, they caught my eye, too, so I thought I might as well…" He shrugged. "You got a vase or something? They probably need some water."

Damn, he thought as he ran water into a tall crystal vase he'd found following her directions, you'd think he was Timmy's age instead of old enough not only to have sown his oats, but harvested the crop.

He put the drinks in the refrigerator, the frozen vegetables that he'd selected by feel and not by label, in the freezer. The doughnuts, he left on the table. "You need more ice on your ankle?" he called.

"I guess so. It's been a while."

"How about something cold to drink? Or I could make coffee."

"Yes to the first two offers, but not the coffee. Did you bring my shoe?"

Jake nearly dropped a tray of ice. Her shoe. He'd left it on the dresser in his bedroom. Like a damned trophy.

Nothing to do but admit it. "Look, I know this is crazy, but I walked right out and forgot the thing. I can go back home right now and get it if—"

She waved him to a chair. "Don't be silly, it's not like I'll be wearing it anytime soon."

"Good thing, too. Shoes like that are just asking for trouble."

Ignoring him, she said, "First I'll have to get the heel repaired."

He shook his head. Women. "Why do you wear those things, anyway?"

"You mean ankle straps?" She batted a set of black eyelashes that had to be at least as long as her red fingernails.

"I mean ten-inch heels." A grin tugged at the corner of his mouth. She was teasing him, and damned if he didn't like it.

"In case you hadn't noticed, I'm slightly height-challenged."

"Short, you mean."

"Well, if you insist on being literal, I'm short and dumpy. And as long as I'm in confession mode, I wasn't born with this shade of hair, either." Laughter trembled on her lips and sparkled through her green contact lenses.

He crooked a grin. "Neither was I. The hair thing."

"You mean you weren't born gray?" she asked, all innocence.

"Believe it or not, I started out as a blond. By the time I was twenty it had turned dark. And yeah, lately the colors have started to change again."

"I started out the color of broom sedge, which is sort of red, I guess. Once I discovered my creative side, I started playing around with colors."

He looked pointedly at her hair. It was currently somewhere between spice-red and maroon and had been cut in varying lengths and gathered up so that it looked carelessly disheveled. "I look ghastly as a brunette," she admitted cheerfully. "I tried several shades of blond, but you know what? I don't care what they say, I never had that much fun as a blonde."

"And fun's the name of the game, right, Ms. Napoleon?"

"Nope. The name of the game is power," she said gravely, and then burst out laughing. "You're fun, did you know that?"

"Oh, yeah—everybody says so. Regular life of the party. Here, let me refill that glass for you." He stood, knowing he should leave before he got in any deeper.

What was it about this woman that made him want to explore every inch of her devious mind?

Her mind. Right.

And that wasn't Jake Smith the private investigator speaking, it was Jake Smith, the man.

She leaned back against a pile of oversize pillows, reminding him of a poster he'd once seen of Mae West. Had the come-up-and-see-me-sometime expression down pat, too.

"Did you play sports in school?" she asked. "Is that where you broke your nose?" Her gaze strayed from his nose to his mouth and back again.

"How'd you know it had been broken?"

"Just a lucky guess. My brother played football. He was a quarterback."

"Pro?"

She shook her head. Her playful look faded. "Just high school. He went to a community college and then joined the sheriff's department. He was killed the first year in an attempted jailbreak."

Jake sagged in his chair. What did you say to something like that? While he was still trying to come up with a response that didn't sound trite, she said, "I'm sorry. You're hardly interested in my family. I don't know why that popped out—frustration, probably. Being stuck here thinking about all the things I need to be doing."

Which made about as much sense as anything else she could come up with, Sasha told herself. The man was like a blotter, inviting all sorts of confidences. If he hung around much longer there was no telling what she might decide to share.

She smoothed her skirt over her knees. After he'd called she had hobbled to the bedroom and changed into a long flower-sprigged yellow skirt and a pale green silk cami—last year's styles, but still flattering. "Do you know many people in Muddy Landing?" she asked brightly.

He hesitated, then said, "I know several deputies— used to know a guy who ran a bait-and-tackle place down on the river. He moved away a few years ago."

"How about your taxes?"

"My what?" He did a double-take.

"Taxes. You know, those things we all have to pay to fund schools and roads and congressmen's junkets?"

"Oh…*those* taxes." He made a face, part amusement, part puzzlement. She was getting so she could almost read him until he put on his detective face. "Yeah, I pay taxes. Property, income, the whole shebang. You need to know how much, I guess I could get you the figures."

Sasha thought he was joking. *Hoped* he was joking. Embarrassed, she hurried to apologize. "I'm sorry, I didn't mean it that way. It's just that I know this CPA who lives not far from here. Her name is Lily Sullivan, and—"

"And?" he said after a while.

She shrugged. And what? For all she knew, Lily had all the business she could handle. For that matter, she might not even be interested in dating. It wouldn't be the first time the trio had goofed. "It's just that I happen to know that she's an excellent CPA, and I thought maybe—" She shook her head. "Forget it. You and your taxes are none of my business."

Rising slowly, Jake towered over her, yet oddly

enough, he wasn't the least bit intimidating. "You want to hand me your corn, I'll put it back in the freezer. Ten minutes, okay? If you've got a cooler I could put it here beside you with a few cold drinks and another bag or two of frozen vegetables."

Embarrassment was her worst enemy. Sasha felt her face growing warm even as she heard herself saying, "No thanks, it's royal blue—my ice chest, that is. I couldn't possibly use it in this room."

He looked at her, and then he looked around the room. "Yeah, now that you mention it, I can see how blue would be a problem."

Obviously, he thought she'd lost her mind. For all she knew, he could be right. "Sorry, I'm not used to being out of action. I tend to get frustrated—my tongue runs away from my brain."

He nodded as if he knew exactly what she was talking about.

Even *she* didn't know just what she was talking about—which was part of the problem.

"You need to stay off that leg as much as possible for at least another day or two. The sooner the swelling goes down, the sooner you can bring your car back home. I don't think it's in too much danger where it is, but you never can tell with a holiday weekend coming up."

She closed her eyes. "Gee, thanks, I really needed that."

"I can have it towed home for you if you're worried. Or if you give me the keys, I can get someone to drive it here for you. Hack—this kid who works with me—"

"No way is any kid named Hack getting his grubby hands on my car," she declared. "Tomorrow I'll have a friend drive me to Kitty Hawk. I'm sure my ankle will be well enough by then."

Jake shifted his weight, wanting to defend his young friend, but then he thought about the rebuilt TR-5 the kid drove. There was probably a reason he'd had a roll bar installed across the top.

He glanced at the flesh-colored bandage, thought about unwrapping it to check the swelling, and backed away, literally and figuratively. Instead of the small metal clip, she had used a gaudy brooch to secure the end. Shaking his head in reluctant admiration, he said, "It's your call. Just remember to pick a time when traffic's light, maybe around supper time or early in the morning."

She nodded and solemnly promised, although they both knew she would do things her way, on her timetable. She'd already proved she wasn't into obeying orders, even when they were in her own best interest.

Stubborn woman, Jake thought half admiringly. Climbing behind the wheel a few minutes later, he told himself to put her out of his mind and get on with his business. He'd done his good deed and that was enough. Hell, he'd even gone the extra mile and brought her flowers.

In exchange, she had screwed up any chance of catching Jamison and his side dish in a compromising situation. He'd tried to call his client, missed her and left a message. He would have liked to have good news—or at least *some* news to report—but as long as that red car was parked outside the cottage, the game was on hold.

Marty and Faylene converged on the lavender house early the next morning. Sasha hobbled to the door to meet them after seeing Marty's white minivan and Faylene's pink Caddie pull up in front of her house.

The night before, she had finally told them about her temporary indisposition, assuring both women that she was on her way to bed and the last thing she wanted was to have to get up and answer the door. That had staved off the visitation until this morning.

"You look bright-eyed and bushy-tailed considering you're just back from your honeymoon," Sasha said, greeting Marty, then laughing, she held up a hand. "No details, please! Just tell me this much—was this one an improvement over the last two?"

Faylene snorted as she strode directly to the kitchen to start a pot of coffee. "Tell you one thing, she's not stopped humming since she got home. 'Nuff to drive a person batty." But her faded blue eyes, set in a bed of wrinkles and frosted turquoise eye shadow, twinkled with amusement.

Five minutes later all three women were seated in the living room with coffee and doughnuts, ready to sift through the local gossip for any snippets that might be useful in their matchmaking games.

Sasha said slyly, "You're obviously getting plenty of sleep." Marty was infamous for her early-morning grumpiness. It was still not quite nine o'clock.

"Quality sleep," the new bride said smugly. "Makes a big difference. And before you take out your crowbar and start prying, that's all I'm saying. So—what's this about a new man for Lily?"

Sasha stirred a second spoonful of sugar into her cup. "He's only perfect, that's all. Like I told you over the phone, he's at least an eleven."

"And that's his shoe size, right?" Marty asked, tongue firmly planted in cheek.

"Uh-uh. His shoes are at least size twelve."

Faylene cackled and Sasha stretched out on the sofa and kicked a pillow under her ankle with her good foot. "Look, I'm just guessing, okay? Lily's tall, right? Jake's taller. He's big, but not too big—attractive without being blatant about it."

"What's wrong with blatant?" asked Faylene, whose Bob Ed was gray-bearded and beer-bellied, and according to the housekeeper, the sweetest man you'd ever hope to meet.

"Well, at least he's not vain. Remember that lawyer we introduced Lily to at the Christmas party? The one who couldn't pass his reflection in any shiny surface without preening?"

"Ask me, I think he used more wax on his hair than he did on his fancy car." Faylene snorted. "And how 'bout the guy that gave her that cheap box of candy that still had the sale sticker on it?"

"Hey, we tried. A good man is hard to find," Sasha said.

"Ain't the way I heard it," Faylene remarked dryly.

"Okay, so the thing is, how are we going to get them together? The box suppers won't start again for another few weeks, and I already asked him about his taxes."

"And?"

"And I botched it. He thought I was being nosy."

"You were, but you're usually slick enough to get away with it," Marty said with a laugh. "You're slipping, honey."

"You try being crafty when your ankle looks like a stuffed sausage and you've got three broken nails on one hand."

"Why don't you go natural? Nobody wears long red nails now. It's not even considered retro. Besides, think of all you'd save in maintenance alone." Marty admired her own French manicure.

"Terrific. Next you'll be wanting me to start wearing gingham."

"I can see it now. A ruffled gingham apron worn over a matching garter belt and bikini top." Marty giggled.

Marty never giggled. Now she not only giggled, she glowed.

Sasha studied her frosted cherry nails—the ones she had left. "Do acrylic nails come in short natural? I told you about my shoe, didn't I? The pink ankle-straps?"

Marty shook her head. "I warned you about those things. This time it was only a sprain, but next time you might break your neck. Shoes like that weren't even meant for walking, much less climbing stairs. And we're talking sun-warped, outdoor stairs with cracks between the boards, right?"

Faylene offered her own advice. "Be like me. I know how to dress sensible for work."

For as long as anyone could remember, the housekeeper's summer uniform had been white sneakers, white shorts and suntan support hose worn, more often than not, with a pink shirt.

"We all have to make the most of our natural attributes. Mine just happen to be small feet, nice ankles and good hair," Sasha said.

"Natural?" Marty jeered. "Yeah, like Mount Rushmore is natural."

"Besides," Sasha continued, ignoring the interruption, "I don't climb all that many stairs. I just had a few more of those three-story cottages this season on account of all the storm damage. And who'd trust a shabby-looking interior designer?"

"We're talking sensible, not shabby. White jeans and a halter, flip-flops and maybe a Hermes do-rag and you've got instant chic."

"Right, and I'd look like every other woman on the beach. Well…maybe not the Hermes scarf." Sasha sighed.

For as long as she could remember she'd loved playing dress-up, her imagination turning her mother's faded cotton dresses into fancy ballgowns. Having been accused more than once of never having met an artifice she didn't like, she'd never bothered to deny it. After dozens of makeovers she had found a style she really liked and stuck to it ever since. And while she might draw the line at silicon and botox, if dewlaps or wattles or cellulite ever seriously threatened, she would definitely go for liposuction—maybe even plastic surgery.

Faylene said, "Long's I'm here, I'll just put in a load of laundry. Be back later this evening to put it in the dryer, so don't you go messin' around in my utility room, y'hear?"

"When did I ever?" Sasha replied.

Marty said, "You know, I've been thinking…that fund-raising yard sale that's coming up? You reckon we could get them together there? There'll be food stands and tables, almost like the box suppers."

"Jake lives in Manteo. He'd hardly come all this way for a local fund-raiser."

"Manteo's not all that far. Besides, it's for an underprivileged kids' summer camp. Betcha he'll go for it if he's as good a guy as you say he is."

"Did I say that?"

In the background, the washing machine began churning.

"You sort of implied," Marty said with a lift of one eyebrow.

"I don't know how you do that." Sasha shook her head. "That one-eyebrow thing."

"It's easy. You could do it, too, if yours were real instead of penciled on."

"Bless her heart," Faylene said, drying her hands on the seat of her shorts as she rejoined them, "It comes from all that waxing she gets done. Last time they slipped up and did her eyebrows along with her legs and I don't know what-all. You get you one o' them Brazilian jobs?"

Sasha tossed a teal-and-orange linen pillow at her. All three women began to giggle, and then the phone rang. Faylene was closest. "Want me to get that?"

"Would you please?"

"Lasiter residence, Faylene speaking."

"Who is it?" Sasha whispered. No matter how many quit-bothering-me lists she signed up for, she still got calls from tour groups, resort salesmen and political surveys.

Faylene held the phone against her pink sequined chest. "Man says his name's Smith. I think it's *him*," she whispered loudly. "He says he's coming this afternoon to take you to get your car." When she hung up, her smirk said it all. "Didn't you say that guy's name was Smith? The one you got picked out for Lily? He sure sounded like a twelve to me. I better go add the softener, I forgot to fill the cup."

"Way to go, gal!" Marty jabbed a fist in the air. "While you've got him here you can tell him about the kids' day-camp fund-raiser and get him on the hook." She gave her a knowing smirk. "Some folks believe in catch-and-release. Me, I never did."

Jake brushed a hand over his newly trimmed hair as he left the barbershop. His client, when he'd finally been able to reach her, had called off the dogs. All a big misunderstanding, according to Ms. J.

Yeah. Sure it was.

All the same, with the holiday weekend bearing down on them, the car wasn't safe where it was.

Which was how Jake came to be driving to Muddy Landing for the second day in a row, neglecting two new commissions, not to mention keeping up with the paint crew that was finishing up work on his side of the duplex. He put it down to a natural talent for procrastination, along with worrying about his son, who was shipping out any day now, and worrying about the Jamison case. Something didn't feel right about it, but at this point it was out of his hands.

He made a mental note to have Miss Martha return the retainer, and then his thoughts veered back along a familiar path.

The phrase, "Out of the frying pan, into the fire," came to mind. He switched on a Molasses Creek CD and tried to focus on the lament of a crabber's woman.

Five

Marty had brought a cold pasta dish earlier and put it in the refrigerator. A size six, Marty had never met a carb she didn't adore. Faylene had brought a can of corned beef hash and a bunch of loose-leaf lettuce from Bob Ed's garden. Her culinary skills were notorious.

So there was no real reason for Sasha to accept Jake's offer of lunch at a seafood restaurant on the way to Kitty Hawk. "I had breakfast early," he said. "Are you sure your ankle's good to go?"

Ignoring the question, she said, "So did I. I'm an early riser."

The truth was, her ankle still bothered her. As for her sleep patterns, those had been crazy for the past three days. Yesterday she had dozed on the sofa during the day, then lain awake half the night. When she finally fell asleep she dreamed.

Oh, how she dreamed…!

Jake had looked her over when she'd first let him in, his gaze moving slowly down her body to settle on her feet. She could have swatted him. For a change, she was wearing one of her few pairs of sensible shoes. Her three-inch cork platforms with flowered straps were the only shoes she could get on over her bandage.

From the way he'd looked at her, she might as well have been wearing stilts.

It had to be her imagination. Too much time on her hands.

After carefully helping her into his SUV, his hands lingered on her arm. He said, "Listen, if you're not up to this, just say so. Like I said, I can get Hack to drive your car to Muddy Landing. It's practically on his way home since he lives in Moyock. The logistics might take some arranging, but we can work it out."

Sasha assured him she was feeling loads better. Actually, she was, until she'd overdone it. Just climbing up and down the stairs was exhausting enough without plowing through the spare room that doubled as a warehouse, looking for the set of framed patent medicine advertisements from a 1920s magazine she'd bought at a yard sale last year. Matted and reframed, they'd be perfect for the suite of doctors' offices she was doing.

They talked shop on the way to Kitty Hawk. Her shop, not his. As it turned out, Jake was a private investigator as well as a security expert. Evidently, private investigators discussed their work only on a need-to-know basis.

It wasn't his work she needed to know about as much as it was the man himself. For all her experience with the opposite sex, she had never met any man who affected her the way this one did. He was sweet, but not smarmy sweet. Sexy without even trying. She could hardly look at him without wondering what he would be like as a lover.

The curse of an inquiring mind!

By the time they were shown to a table in the beach-front restaurant, Sasha was practically salivating, which wasn't like her at all. It must be a lingering side effect of the painkillers she'd taken the first day and then dumped.

Once seated, she announced to the waitress, "I'll start with dessert. Then, if I'm still hungry, I might have something healthy. Lemon chess pie, please."

Jake looked at her across the table, scattering her feeble defenses with a lazy grin. "Why am I not surprised?"

Judging from the looks the waitress was giving him, Sasha wasn't the only one who'd like a large serving of Jake.

Without even glancing at the menu he ordered the fried oyster basket. She opened her mouth to ask if it was true what they said about oysters, then closed it before she could make a fool of herself. Any more of a fool, that was.

"You were serious," he said after the waitress left. "About having dessert first."

She fluttered a battery of false lashes. "I'm always serious."

He stared at her. She fluttered again. And then they both started laughing. "Don't make me wrinkle my eyes," she protested, "these things aren't foolproof."

"You mean those centipedes circling your eyes aren't real?"

"Absolutely, they're real. They're the best money can buy, but the glue's not guaranteed against squinting or crying."

Jake shook his head admiringly and Sasha preened. Flirtation was a game she always won, even though the prize was rarely worth the effort.

"Coffee with the pie, Miss?" Plopping the plate down in front of her, the waitress addressed Sasha while she looked ready to melt all over Jake. Sasha found it irritating in the extreme. With all the bronzed, sun-bleached surfers running around with their trunks at half-mast, what was so hot about a fully dressed guy with laugh lines, squint lines, and a sparkling of gray?

Sasha sighed. Jake nodded. "Bring her a decaf."

She waited until the girl left and then said, "I never drink decaf."

"You need to decompress. About your car—it's a little soon, so if you're not up to driving yet, we could—"

"I'm perfectly capable of driving." She was a big girl now; she could stand a little pain.

"Do you have an alarm?"

"A car alarm? I had one, but it got to be such an annoyance I had it disabled."

"An annoyance how?"

"It went off every time I forgot to click the little whoosie."

Jake sighed. And then he grinned. "Lady, you need a keeper."

"Thanks, but I already tried that. Four times, in fact."

He choked on a swallow of ice water. "Four times you did *what?*"

"Four times I thought I'd found a keeper, only I ended up having to throw him back."

He took a few seconds to process her claim. "You mean you had four, uh—relationships? That's not too surprising, I guess. Be more surprising if you hadn't." All the same, he looked as if he'd bitten into a particularly sour pickle.

"Not relationships. Husbands."

He shook his head slowly, but said nothing. The waitress brought Jake's oysters and looked questioningly at Sasha, who was only half finished with her pie. "I should have ordered it à la mode. Anything this sweet needs to be diluted with ice cream." When the girl continued to hover uncertainly, she said, "Oh, I guess you can bring me a salad. Any kind—just something disgustingly healthy."

She should have known Jake wasn't going to let her off the hook that easily. Once the waitress left, he leaned forward, forcing Sasha to look at him. "Now repeat what you just said. You've had four *husbands?*"

She did the eyelash thing again, trying for a look of innocence, but he was on to her now. "You make me sound like Lizzie Borden, or that Borgia woman. I didn't kill anybody, I just divorced them." She tilted her head to one side. "Why are you looking at me like that? I made four mistakes, okay? What's wrong, haven't you ever made a mistake?"

"More than my share, I just never married 'em."

"Then you're not married?"

"I was once, but it was no mistake. Rosemary was the best thing that ever happened to me. If it weren't for her, I wouldn't have my son."

She looked at him wistfully. "You have a son. You're incredibly lucky, but I guess you know that. I've always wanted one."

Jake accepted the remark with a nod. Then he started to ask her why she'd never had kids with any of her four husbands, but decided it was none of his business. Besides, it was hardly the sort of question a man asked of a woman he'd known casually for only a few days. A woman he had no intention of getting to know any better.

"Tell me about him—your son." She touched her lips with the napkin and crumpled it beside her plate.

Why not? Jake thought. It was safer than talking about what really interested him, such as why none of the men she'd married had been able to hang on to her. "I could start by saying he's everything any man could want in a son." His gaze moved past her shoulder to a wide, salt-filmed window, where a glimpse of the ocean could be seen between the dunes. "I just wish he weren't heading overseas."

Knowing she was staring at him, he tried to erase any hint of what he was thinking, but it was probably already too late.

"I told you about my brother," she reminded him quietly.

Jake nodded. For some crazy reason he found himself wanting to confide in her. To share not only his pride, but his very real worries. He'd never been the kind of guy who opened up to every stranger who came along. Besides, they weren't even friends. His mother would probably have labeled her fast, any woman who'd been married and divorced four times.

His grandmother would have called her a hussy, a painted lady—maybe even a scarlet woman.

The trouble was, Jake had a feeling that under all that paint and polish there lurked a very different kind of woman. A woman with weaknesses and vulnerabilities she tried a little too hard to conceal. One his mother and even his grandmother would probably like if they ever got to know her.

"You want more coffee?" he asked, reaching for any safe topic.

"Did I mention that I have twin sisters, too? Annette and Jeanette. They're almost ten years younger than I am and both happily married, with children." She waited a beat and added, "One husband apiece, in case you were wondering. We don't all run to multiple unions. Mama remarried after Daddy died, but then, she was barely fifty at the time. Her new husband raises llamas out in Colorado. He's gentle as a lamb."

All of which was far more than he needed to know, Jake mused, but judging from the way it had come out, like a faucet turned on full-blast, she'd needed to tell him. Odd comment, though—that part about her step-father being gentle as a lamb.

"The only trouble is, they all live so far away," she said with a sigh. "Anne lives in Birmingham, Jeanie in Tampa. I haven't seen either of them in more than a year." She toyed with her fork, making tiny squares in the sticky stuff on her pie plate. "And you know what's so funny? Now that I'm finally in a position to help, they don't need me anymore." She rolled her eyes, a look of disgust on her face. "That sounded so awful. Can I please take back my whine?"

Jake started to laugh, but didn't. He started to say something—God knows what—when his cell phone vibrated at his waist. One glance at the number and he swallowed hard. Timmy was probably calling to say goodbye. His unit had been day-to-day ever since their orders came down.

"Excuse me, will you?" he murmured.

Meaning to go the ladies' room and allow him some privacy, Sasha started to stand, grabbed the chair back when her ankle protested, and plopped down again. Instead, she reached for her half-eaten pie, pretending a fascination with the too-sweet confection while she tried not to listen.

A long pause and then, "Jesus, son, this is—"

Son? This was Timmy, then, not a business call. And Jake was frowning. Sasha's mind immediately manufactured a dozen possibilities, all of them tragic. At least the boy was able to call—that was a good sign. But if Jake's brows lowered any more, he wouldn't be able to see.

Her pie was suddenly tasteless, the crust leathery. She took a sip of her tasteless coffee only to find it was barely warm. Murmuring an excuse, she started to rise again just as he said, "What if I talk to your commanding officer?"

Oh, God, this was serious! Could the boy have been arrested? Had he deserted? Going AWOL—that was a court-martial offense, wasn't it?

"All right, give me her name and tell me how to get in touch with her. I'll call you back as soon as I know something positive. Within the hour if I'm lucky—I'm on the beach, not too far away."

His commanding officer was a woman. Did that help or hurt? Sasha was undecided whether to disappear, ignore the call or ask if there was anything she could do to help. She knew two county commissioners personally, but they probably didn't have a whole lot of clout with the military.

"Don't worry, son, I'll handle it. You just keep your head down and your mind on what you're supposed to be doing. Leave everything else to me."

He shut off the cell phone, laid it on the table and stared blindly at a salt shaker for a full minute—a minute during which Sasha ran through every possible way in which a teenage boy, even if he was a soldier, could get in trouble. "Can I help?" she finally asked.

"I should have given him a refresher course, like maybe about nine months ago." Rising, he pulled out his wallet and tossed several bills on the table.

Sasha wasn't about to mention her car, which happened to be in the opposite direction, nor was she about to ask any questions. From the look on his face, he had enough on his mind without adding her tiny problems.

Not until they turned off the bypass and headed toward one of the older soundside villages did Jake break the silence. Dropping back to the slower speed limit, he drove past several small houses, a few of which looked as if they hadn't been repaired since Hurricane Isabel. "She says she needs the money because she hasn't been able to work for the past few months."

She? Who was *she?* And what did she have to do with Jake's son? More to the point, what did she have to do with Jake?

Questions swarmed like a school of minnows, but as much as she wanted to help, she hesitated to pry into his personal business.

Jake slowed down to check a street marker. "Here's

what I don't get," he said as if they were in the middle of a conversation. "She didn't ask him for money. Didn't ask for a damn thing, she just said she wanted to let him know what happened and what she planned to do about it." He turned right and cruised down a narrow black-top street at about five miles an hour.

Looking as pale as a perennially suntanned man could possibly look, he swore softly under his breath. "She waited five and a half weeks to call him—five and a half damned weeks! Tim said he told her that as long as she'd waited that long, to hold off until he talked to me. I just hope to God she did—that she's still there."

He obviously didn't expect a response. In fact, Sasha wasn't certain he realized she was even here. If he was working things out in his own mind, the last thing he needed was questions—although sometimes a sounding board could help.

"You know what?" he asked suddenly, still without looking at her. "I'm not buying it. Tim said they spent last Labor Day weekend together at Virginia Beach, but he claims he hasn't seen her since then. I've never known him to lie, not even when a lie would have gotten him out of trouble."

"They've obviously been in touch," Sasha ventured. "She knew where to find him." She still wasn't quite certain what the problem was, but she was beginning to think it had nothing to do with the military. Evidently, Timmy and an old girlfriend had a problem. And now Jake was involved.

They passed a shoebox with weathered siding and tarpaper patches on the roof, and then Jake backed up, pulled off the pavement and opened the driver's-side door. Near the wooden steps an enormous gardenia bush in full bloom layered the air with its fragrance.

"You want to wait out here?"

It was the first time he'd actually acknowledged her presence. "Can you give me a quick rundown on what's going on? If this is a hostage situation, I'd just as soon wait outside, but I'll keep the car running in case you need to make a quick getaway."

Still holding the door open, Jake leaned back in his seat and closed his eyes. "Sorry. Communication's obviously not one of my skills. In a nutshell, my son impregnated a girl last Labor Day weekend. They've talked a few times since, but Tim says he hasn't seen her since then. Five and a half weeks ago she had a baby and she swears it's his."

"Do you think she's telling the truth?"

Jake's shoulders drooped. Suddenly he looked his age. It should have diminished his sex appeal, yet oddly enough, it didn't. She wanted nothing more than to gather him into her arms and offer comfort. In whatever form he preferred.

Girl, you just never learn, do you?

"Short answer—yes, I think she's probably telling the truth."

"Why is that?"

"Like I said, she didn't ask for anything—no money, no wedding ring. She was just reporting in, letting him know what she planned to do. According to Tim, she's been talking with a woman in Norfolk who takes unwanted babies and places them in good homes."

"You mean an adoption agency?"

He shrugged. "I guess. Probably a private one. Tim

made her hold off until he could get in touch with me. He's in no position to take care of a baby. Hell, neither am I, for that matter, but I'll tell you this much—nobody is going to sell my granddaughter."

"How long do we have?"

He turned to her then. "There's no 'we' about it. There's me and this woman and my granddaughter. Look, Sasha, I'm sorry about all this—the delay. I promise you, once I get things settled here, I'll see that you get to your car."

"Oh, bull pucky!"

For the first time since he'd received the call from his son, Jake looked almost amused. "*Pucky?* I haven't heard that one, is it original?"

"I doubt it. My daddy started out as a farmer. Once he switched to preaching, we all had to clean up our language."

"Yeah, well…while I go inside, how about making a list of everything I need to buy to take care of a baby. Diapers, bottles—a car seat."

He swung open his door, then turned and said, "Dammit, didn't those kids ever hear of birth control? Tim says she was seventeen when he knew her. That's barely legal."

As if knowing she wasn't going to stay put, he came around just as she opened the door and started to slide to the ground. Catching her, he steadied her against his chest, holding her closely for a moment as if he needed the brief contact as much as she did.

"Four-wheel-drive SUVs aren't designed with the vertically challenged in mind," she said breathlessly as she backed away. The man generated enough voltage to jump-start a battleship.

Leading the way across the unkempt yard to the shoebox house, he said gruffly, "Come on, let's get this show on the road."

They stepped up onto the porch where two pairs of sandy flip-flops straddled a potted tomato plant. Sasha caught his arm and said, "Look, this might be out of line, but just so you know, I have lots of money."

The look he gave her might have withered her on the spot if she didn't know how concerned he was. Turning away, he jabbed the buzzer and then rattled the screen door. From inside the house came the sound of a radio playing loud rap music. Jake's look darkened.

Sasha said, "You were expecting what, lullabies? Mother or not, she's still a teenager."

The girl who materialized on the other side of the mended screen looked as if she could do with a few pounds, a few hours in the sun and a few hours of sleep.

"I'm Tim's dad. He told you I'd be here. Where is she?"

The young woman looked them over thoroughly before she opened the screen door. "I guess you might as well come in. Is this Tim's mother?"

"I'm a friend," Sasha answered before Jake could explain that she was practically a stranger who just happened to come along for the ride. "Could we see her?"

"She spit up and I've not had time to change her shirt."

She led the way to a room that was even more depressing than the one they were in, and there in the middle of an unmade bed was a banana box stuffed with a pillow. Tiny pink feet kicked at a confining yellow spread. A small pink fist waved in the air as a red-faced infant vented her displeasure.

"That's her. I named her Tuesday on account of that's when she was born. Tuesday Smith," she added defiantly.

"And your name is?" said Jake, who looked tense enough to shatter at a touch.

"Cheryl," was the reluctant response. "Cheryl Moser."

Torn between reaching out to Jake and scooping up the fretful infant, Sasha chose the safest option. She leaned over and cupped a small foot in her hand. "Hello, sweetheart. You just fuss all you want to, I don't much blame you." She turned to the tired-looking blonde. "How old did you say she was?"

"Five weeks. And a half."

Jake said tightly, "You could have called sooner."

"I didn't think you'd be interested."

"What about your parents?"

She shrugged. "Mama's dead and Daddy said don't come crying to him if I got myself in trouble."

Sasha opened her mouth and then shut it again. Nothing she could say would help out in this situation. This was between Jake and the thin, pale teenager and a baby whose name was the same as a movie star this poor girl had probably never heard of. So much for originality.

Frowning, Jake said, "About this place in Norfolk—"

Sasha broke in. "Whatever that woman offered, we'll double it." She hadn't planned to say anything, the words just popped out.

Jake shot her a look that clearly questioned her sanity. To Cheryl, he said, "Why don't we go in the next room and talk this over?"

Not to be left out, Sasha scooped the infant from her makeshift bassinet, making crooning sounds she hadn't uttered in more than twenty years, and followed them into the living room, carrying the wet, fussing infant against her shoulder. Oh, how good it felt to cradle a baby again.

Jake turned to glare at her. Cheryl sighed and shifted her weight from one bare foot to the other. "Look, I mean, I just need to get back to work full-time, okay? Starting when I got too big to work tables, they put me in the kitchen. The pay stinks. I been taking her with me, but my boss don't like it. How much did you say you were willing to give for her?"

On the verge of saying something she probably shouldn't, Sasha felt a warm damp patch on the shoulder of her eighty-nine-dollar-on-sale, dry-cleanable blouse. It smelled like sour milk and probably was. "Judge not lest ye be judged" had been one of the favorite quotations of Addler Parrish, who had set himself up as judge and then proceeded to mete out whatever punishment he saw fit.

She'd been nine and a half when the twins were born, eleven when her brother came along. Her mother had been sickly after Buck, whose real name had been Robert, so Sasha had done more than her share of baby-tending. The warmth of the slight bundle and the familiar smell brought back a mixture of bitterness and nostalgia.

Speaking in a quietly controlled voice, Jake named a figure. While Cheryl gnawed on a hangnail, evidently considering his offer, Sasha cleared her throat loudly. When Jake glanced at her she waggled her eyebrows to remind him that she had money if his offer wasn't enough.

She knew very well she had no business meddling in his affairs, but the only thing that mattered here was this baby. If there was anything she could do to help smooth the way, she intended to do it, no matter whose toes she stepped on.

The baby whimpered, and she held her up and sniffed at her diaper. "Where do you keep her things? I can change her for you—her shirt, too."

"She spits up all the time. Over there." The girl pointed to a scarred table that held a folded towel, two packages of disposable diapers, a tin of baby powder and a half-empty nursing bottle.

"Come on, sugar pie, let Sasha make you feel better, hmm?"

Humming under her breath, she located the pitifully small stack of undershirts and took care of business while trying to overhear the negotiations going on in the next room. Cheryl was insisting loudly that the baby was definitely Tim's, and to prove it she'd put his name on the birth certificate.

Jake, in a voice even more controlled than before, said, "I'm not questioning your word. If you'd asked him for money or a wedding ring, I might've have had my doubts, but since you didn't ask for anything, I'll give you credit for playing it straight."

Reentering the living room, Sasha thought of the twins and how lucky they'd been to marry decent men the first time around. They could easily have ended up in the same situation as this poor girl.

The baby was trying to cram Sasha's finger in her mouth. "Oh, honey, sapphires don't taste all that good—this one's not even real. Let's find you a pacifier, hmm?"

Just then Jake spelled out his terms, naming a generous figure. "I'll write you a check for half today—I've got a checkbook out in the truck. You'll get the other half once we get things wrapped up legally."

"Look, I already told you, I'll sign whatever you want me to sign." She sounded close to tears.

Sasha thought that of all the painful things a woman could do, giving up her baby had to be among the worst. Cradling the infant, she said, "I know you want what's best for her."

Cheryl turned to Jake. "You're her granddaddy. You'll take care of her and nobody would try to take her away from you, would they?"

Sasha waited to hear his reply. He might be an expert in his field, but outnumbered by emotional females in a room that smelled of baby powder, soiled diapers and sour milk, he was obviously out of his element.

He fished out his wallet, extracted a card and wrote his cell-phone number on the back. "Here—you can see her anytime you want to once we get things settled, as long as you call first. You'll get the rest of your money as soon as we meet with the lawyer, but I'm taking her with me now."

"Today? Can't I get the rest of my money today?"

"I doubt if I can get an appointment that soon, but—"

"I can," Sasha said.

They both turned to her. "Let me make a call. This lawyer I know owes me a big favor for getting him—well, never mind that. He specializes in real estate, but considering nobody's contesting the adoption, it should be enough to get by on, don't you think?"

Later she would wonder how in the world she'd gotten involved in the matter, but at no time could she have stepped away. Blame it on missing her own family, remembering the time when Buck and the twins had depended on her. Blame it on the hopes she'd once had of having children of her own.

"Sasha's got you now, sweetheart. You're going to be just fine, you wait and see," she whispered.

Six

"Well, that went pretty well, don't you think?" Sasha leaned forward from the back of the car, one hand on the infant car seat that was secured with a seatbelt.

Neither Jake nor Cheryl said a word. After explaining the situation to the lawyer, they'd spent less than an hour in his office. Jake and Cheryl had signed an agreement, with Sasha serving as a witness. The small act of signing her name on little Miss Tuesday no-middle-name Smith's adoption papers had set her eyes to watering. Jake had written two checks, one for the lawyer and one for a tearful Cheryl.

The drive back to the house on Low Ridge Road where the young woman lived was largely silent. As they pulled up in front of the house, Jake said quietly, "Starting today I'll be putting money into her college fund."

Sasha thought that was probably as reassuring as

anything he could possibly have said. She hadn't missed Cheryl's occasional sniffle. And while her heart ached for the girl now, she had an idea that Cheryl Moser was a survivor.

While Jake got out and came around to the passenger side, Sasha whispered, "Call me if you ever need someone to talk to. I have two younger sisters." Granted, the twins were a lot older than Cheryl, but the sentiment still held. "That's up to you, but Jake's a wonderful man—he'll take good care of her, you'll never have to worry about that."

Just before Jake returned from seeing the young woman to her door, she carefully blotted her eyes with a tissue. It came away smudged with black and taupe.

Oh, well, she thought, resigned. It's not as if he hadn't seen her in even worse shape. "We'll probably need to make a stop at the nearest outfitters," she said. Except for the basics, Cheryl had improvised. Even the diaper bag was a battered canvas beach tote.

Heading for the closest big-box store, Jake picked up the conversation that had been left dangling earlier. "If the father hadn't been my son, I doubt if things would've gone that smoothly."

"If the father hadn't been your son," Sasha reminded him dryly, "you wouldn't have been there in the first place." She wondered if he had any idea of how many changes were in store for him over the next few days, not to mention the next few years. Granted, he'd once had a baby, but he'd been younger then. Besides, he'd had someone to share the responsibility. Whether or not he realized it, his whole life had just undergone a dramatic change.

She admitted to herself that she envied him with all her heart.

Jake switched on the radio. When static crackled noisily, he switched it off again and said something about lightning.

Lightning my hind foot, Sasha thought. His touch was enough to short out any radio. She knew from experience that there was enough voltage in that tall, muscular frame to light up a small town. Idly, she wondered what it would be like to plug into all that current.

To plug into it? Oh, for Pete's sake, quit with the visuals!

"Timmy will be so proud of you," she said as they pulled into the vast parking lot. "Why don't you try to call him while I shop?"

"You need some money." He shifted his hips and reached for his wallet, and she shook her head.

"We'll settle up later. I don't know if I can get anything but the basics here."

He looked startled. "The basics?"

She left him staring after her. Oh, honey, you have so much to learn, she thought, and I'm just the one who can teach you. That is, if I can stay ahead of the learning curve.

Maybe she'd better look for an instruction book for new parents while she was at it.

Some forty-five minutes later Sasha pushed a loaded cart to the car. She was followed by another cart pushed by a clerk. On the way to the SUV where Jake and the baby waited, she smiled, thinking about how much fun it was going to be, unloading the booty and setting up a nursery. "Thank you so much," she said to the middle-aged employee who had been an enormous help. She plucked a bill from her purse and shoved it into the woman's red apron pocket.

"Oh, now, you don't have to do that—I'm just glad I could help out."

Sasha, never reticent, had told the woman the whole story when she'd asked for her assistance, leaving out only the names. When Jake, who'd been standing beside the open back door, turned to meet them, the clerk flashed Sasha a broad smile and whispered, "Lawsamercy, he don't look like a grandfather to me!"

Ignoring the departing clerk, Jake stared at the two overloaded shopping carts. Before he could say a word, Sasha rushed into speech. "We'll need to get a few more things later on. I got us the same kind of formula Cheryl was using, and a complete layette with lots and lots of diapers—oh, and this funky little chest to keep everything in. And a bathtub. Later on we'll need a table for bathing and changing unless you already have something, but the only one they had was too rickety. The bassinet came in two colors and white. I got white so it would go with whatever color you paint the nursery. They had a larger one, but since she'll be graduating to a crib pretty soon anyway, I thought…"

Jake blinked as if he suspected the two overloaded shopping carts were a mirage that had magically appeared in the middle of the parking lot. "Really," Sasha hurried to reassure him, "it's not as much as it looks— you know how they over-package everything. And I kept the receipts so we can return anything that doesn't work out."

For so long she'd dreamed of having a baby of her own, but that was before fate and her own bad taste in husbands had laid the dream to rest. Now, even with the perfect mate, her chances of conceiving were less than the odds of the Cubs winning the World Series again.

But even a patched-up dream with some of the parts missing was better than no dream at all, she told herself.

There was still the question of her car. Driftwinds cottage was just a few miles away, but when Jake mentioned it she told him to forget it. "You need me to help you get settled," Sasha said flatly, climbing into the back seat. "Did she wake up? Did you get too hot in here, sugar? Oh—that's probably why you left the back door open, isn't it?"

Jake growled something she couldn't quite catch, and she thought, Ah-ha! Caught you! You left it open just to look at her, to admire her—to gloat, because she's yours now, didn't you?

Aloud, she said, "She might be hungry—she's probably wet, too. I don't remember if I got any diaper-rash ointment or not, but we can stop by the nearest drugstore."

"Sasha, you don't have to come with me—with us. You've already done more than enough."

"Oh, hush up, whether or not you want to admit it, I'm already part of this whole baby deal. My name's on her adoption papers, remember?"

Jake raked his hand through his hair, looking distracted, worried, and incredibly sexy. Without giving him time to marshal his thoughts, she said, "Look, I'll just help you get everything set up and then I'll call a cab to bring me back to Kitty Hawk to pick up my car."

She knew it wouldn't be that simple. Jake probably did, too, but to her relief, he didn't argue. Poor man, he was so far out of his element he was putty in her hands.

Don't I wish, she thought longingly.

While she was shopping she'd bought herself an inexpensive tank top that was really rather nice, and changed into it in the ladies' room. Maybe she should shop the discount stores more often. Her friends had been telling her that for years, which made her do exactly the opposite.

She was supposed to have style, for Pete's sake— she was an interior designer. Who wanted a designer who bought her clothes from the same store her housekeeper did?

Jake said gruffly, "Sit up front, we need to talk."

Uh-oh, here's where I get dumped, Sasha told herself.

But they headed south toward Manteo, which meant he wasn't going to drop her off at Driftwinds. Not yet, anyway. She waited for him to speak, and when he didn't, she said, "What are we going to call her?" Neither of them particularly cared for the name on her birth certificate. "What was your mother's name?"

He pulled up at a traffic light. "Rebecca," he replied, tapping the steering wheel.

"That's nice. If she doesn't like it she can change it when she grows up. I did."

He cut her a quick glance. "Changed your name? What'd you start out with?"

"Sally June." She shrugged. "Once I grew up, it just wasn't me."

He smiled at that. It was the first smile she'd seen in hours. Evidently he was coming out of his state of shock. "Yeah, you're probably right. How'd you come by the name Sasha?"

Twisting around, she glanced at the back seat. "All's peaceful. She's just looking around and blinking. I think she's sleepy again. My name? I read it in a book. I've always been a reader, even when I had to hide my books in the barn or under my mattress."

"You read *that* kind of books?" He looked amused, which made him look younger than she'd first thought. She'd placed his age at a year or two more than her own—possibly even less, considering that he'd obviously spent most of it outdoors, probably without the benefit of sunscreen or moisturizers.

But they'd been talking about books, not the texture of his face, with those squint lines and laugh lines, and the afternoon shadow of beard that cried out to be stroked. So she said, "I read every kind of book I could get my hands on, usually at ten cents a copy from yard sales. The only trouble was, there weren't that many yard sales in our neighborhood. People tended to hang on to whatever they owned until it wore out." She made it sound like a joke. It wasn't. She'd grown up dirt-poor, which probably explained her present lifestyle.

"There's always the backs of cereal boxes." They cruised along at the speed of traffic, which was erratic at best. Jake was an excellent driver, anticipating trouble before she was even aware of it. "Or don't kids still read those?"

"Once you've read a few oatmeal boxes, you know how the story ends."

He smiled again. That was twice in the past few minutes. Sasha glanced at him, seeing the furrows between his eyebrows disappear while the ones bracketing his mouth grew deeper. This is why I knew I had to come with him, she thought. He *needs* me. He might not be ready to admit it, but he really does need me.

He could've dropped her off at her car when they'd left the restaurant. It would have taken only a few more minutes. Instead, he'd taken her with him to find Cheryl.

He could have driven her to Driftwinds and left her there after they'd seen the lawyer, or after she'd done his shopping for him. Instead, he was taking her home with him. That had to mean something.

Dream on, she mocked silently. The trouble with being a Libra was that she was heavily under the influence of Venus. Venus people weren't exactly known for their common sense.

Somewhere between the seventh and the ninth milepost, Jake's frown reappeared. Shooting her a helpless look—or at least, as helpless as a big, sexy guy in the prime of life could manage—he said, "Back to names— I thought maybe I'd let Timmy suggest one if he doesn't care for Tuesday. I talked to him while you were in the store, but we didn't get around to discussing names."

"That's fine, but what do we call her now?"

"Does it matter? I doubt if she understands the language yet."

"You'd be surprised what babies pick up on. For instance, if she gets the least idea you feel uncomfortable with her, she has ways of expressing herself that you're probably not going to like, especially in the middle of the night."

"Hey, I'm not exactly a novice. I had a baby once. I don't remember Tim being all that much trouble."

"That's because you had a wife to deal with colic and night feedings. Peaches is going to demand a lot of attention. You sure you're up to it?"

"Peaches? Is food the only thing you can think about? You should have eaten your lunch." The look he gave her was partly amusement, partly irritation.

"She has a dimple in her chin, did you notice? She probably got that from you." His was a shallow cleft, not a dimple, but connections were important. "And I guess you know her eyes might not stay the same color." Jake's were hazel. "Most babies, at least the ones in my family, are born with blue eyes. It's hard to tell about her hair, considering how little she has now, but I'll bet anything it will be curly. People with dimples in their chins often have curly hair. I read that somewhere."

Jake cut her off. In a dawn of understanding, he said slowly, "My God. You *want* her. Admit it, you want my baby!"

In the silence that followed his astonishing conclusion, Sasha couldn't come up with a single credible denial. If ever there had been a point at which she could have walked away from Jake Smith, regardless of the baggage he carried, that point had passed. Now that she was involved up to her zircon-studded ears, it was too late. Her reaction when he'd accused her of wanting his baby was a pretty good indication of just how "too-late," it was.

Darn right she wanted his baby. But logical or not, she wanted to have it the old-fashioned way, with both of them hot, naked and trembling with urgency. If they both tried long enough and hard enough, maybe a miracle would happen.

She stole a glance at his profile. Not once in their brief relationship had he given her any real indication that he was interested in her as a woman.

Oh, well…maybe once or twice. There was the way he'd looked at her while he was carrying her down several flights of stairs, and when he'd lifted her out of his SUV to take her inside the hospital. He'd caught his breath, his eyes had darkened, and then he'd caught it again. Probably her perfume. It was an old classic that was extremely hard to find, but well worth the effort.

On the other hand, he might have just pulled a muscle in his back.

At any rate, the fact that he'd driven all the way back to Muddy Landing to check on her the next day proved what a nice man he was.

Unfortunately, it wasn't his "niceness" she was interested in.

Well, it was—but that was icing on the cake. Whatever it was that set her imagination, not to mention her hormones, to spinning like a tipsy gyroscope, was more than merely physical—although the physical alone was enough to blow out a few vital circuits in her brain. She'd been in lust before, but this was different. It had nothing to do with any fancy pheromone-based cologne. Those, she had no trouble resisting.

It had nothing to do with the way he dressed. He obviously wasn't out to make a fashion statement with designer silk shirts open to show off his manly chest or Italian slacks cleverly tailored to show off the "package." His package didn't need enhancing. Regardless of what he was wearing, he was more than enough to cause a major meltdown.

And dammit, she wanted him to do more than *need* her, she wanted him to *want* her! To look at her and wonder where she'd been all his life. To know the instant she walked into a room even if it was pitch-dark and he couldn't see her. To *know*.

She wasn't a romance writer; she couldn't describe the feeling—but any woman who had ever fallen in love would know exactly what she meant.

They drove past another shopping center and Sasha tried to think of anything she might have forgotten, but she was too distracted by the hectic pace of events over the past few hours.

Why was it, she wondered as they crossed over the Washington Baum Bridge, that this particular man affected her in ways that none of the men she'd married had even come close to? Both her first and her third husbands had been more handsome. In fact, Larry had spent more than she did on salon treatments at a time when they could barely afford to pay the rent.

Frank, her fourth husband, had been richer—the jerk. At least he'd been generous…sort of. For every thousand dollars he'd spent on his own back, he'd lavished a few hundred on hers. It hadn't been enough, though—not nearly enough once she'd learned where the money had come from.

As they took a right and turned into Manteo, she was still wondering how an accidental meeting could have led to—well, to whatever this thing was that she was involved in now.

Once upon a time she used to sleep in one of her mother's old T-shirts. The thing was faded almost colorless, but the flower-entwined words Go with the Flow had still been legible across the front. When she'd asked what it meant, her mother had murmured tiredly, "Oh, honey, it don't mean anything. Just some old silliness people used to say back when I was young and foolish."

Instead of going with the flow, Sasha, who'd been Sally June back then, had insisted on swimming against the current. By the time she'd bought her house in Muddy Landing and settled down just a few miles from the beach, she knew the old mantra had nothing to do with the ocean tides. And while she didn't personally buy into the philosophy of every feel-good guru to hit the bestseller charts, she always tried to keep an open mind.

Was it too big a stretch to believe that this thing between her and Jake was one of those fate-engineered relationships? Considering all that had happened over the past few days, it definitely had the earmarks. In which case, ignoring it would be asking for trouble.

Go with the flow. If the saying had originated about the time she'd been born, she might even have been conceived at one of those love-in things her mother used to talk about back before her father had given up on farming and gotten religion. Tattered tents and VW buses with daisies and peace symbols painted all over them, guitars and penny whistles—free love and shared grass…

For all she knew she might even be a reincarnated hippie.

Probably not, though. The age was all wrong, and besides, she detested baggy, patched jeans, hairy legs and flapping boots. Especially on women.

Sasha took a deep breath as they cruised slowly down Manteo's Main Street. If this was a fate-engineered thing, then fate had better get busy fast, because once

Jake got home with his baby, she would probably never see either of them again.

Just then Jake pulled into a fast-food place. Without consulting her, he ordered bacon cheeseburgers and fries for two. Sasha inhaled the fragrance of hot grease and realized that she was starved.

Back off, fate, we've got ourselves a time-out.

"We can eat after we get home. Won't be but a few more minutes," he said, and then he frowned.

"Problem?" she asked.

"What? Oh, no. Maybe. I forgot."

"You forgot what? Whether or not you have a problem?" When he started to swear, she shushed him. "Don't imprint her innocent little mind."

"Ah, jeez… Look, Sasha, I just remembered something. It might not be so bad, but I'd better see how long it's going to take to finish."

With that cryptic remark he turned left onto Burnside, took a right and another left and pulled up in front of a duplex. A modest sign identified it as JBS Security. One of the two front doors was propped open and two shirtless men hammered on the roof. A workman with a paint-spattered beard emerged from the door on the left carrying a ladder, which he left on the front porch.

Jake said, "They were supposed to be finished today." He sounded tired. He sounded frustrated. It was all she could do not to pat his hand and say something helpful alike, "There, there."

"Can you and, uh—Peaches wait here? I'll just be a minute."

Less than five minutes later he came out again and asked if she needed a pit stop. More from curiosity than need, she said she could use one. He said, "Come on, then—I'll take the baby. I can check my messages and make a couple of calls."

So she got to meet his staff, including Miss Martha, the gray-haired secretary, and Hack, who might be an electronics genius but she would never trust him anywhere near her wheels, not on a bet.

Naturally, they had to hear the whole story. Jake sketched in the bare bones, then disappeared behind a freshly painted closed door, leaving Sasha to fill in the details. Which she did, starting with Timmy's call and ending up with the official documentation, which might or might not stand up in court if it were ever challenged.

"Well, I never," the older woman marveled. "You did the right thing. I'd like to see the judge who'd rule against one of our boys in uniform."

Hack went back to whatever he'd been working on, while Miss Martha admired the baby. "Got your grandpa's chin, haven't you, precious? It's like something you see in one of those reality shows everybody watches nowadays."

Sasha didn't watch those. She preferred her own version of reality to anything manufactured for TV. "I think her eyes are going to stay blue, don't you?"

"Our Timmy's eyes are the prettiest blue you ever saw." The two women beamed down at the infant, who seemed mesmerized, but probably wasn't. Sasha tried and failed to remember just when babies started focusing. It had been so long….

"We'll probably see plenty of her once Jake gets finished with the painting next door," Martha Blount murmured. "We did the office first. He's been sleeping in his office." She nodded toward the door behind which he'd disappeared. "There's room in there for a bassinet...or I could take her home with me and bring her to work every morning."

"We've already made arrangements," Sasha lied.

Jake emerged from his office sweating and muttering.

Miss Martha said, "Hush up, Jake. Little pitchers have big ears."

Hack glanced up from his work table and said, "Forgot to tell you, boss—I took the air-conditioning apart to see what was making that racket."

When the baby started to whimper, Miss Martha said, "If you've got a bottle ready—"

Not waiting to hear the rest, Sasha dashed out to the car and retrieved the needed supplies. If Peaches was hungry now she needed feeding now.

"Look, you've got problems," she said to Jake a few minutes later. Putting the baby to her shoulder, she said, "Why don't I just call a cab and take sweety-britches here home with me. You can bring the rest of her stuff later after you get off work. Or maybe tomorrow." Can't blame a woman for trying.

"Just sit tight, I'll be done here in a minute," Jake muttered.

Ten minutes later they were on the way north again. "Everything all right?" she asked quietly.

"Fine," he snapped.

Uh-huh. "Then what was all the fuss about back there?" she asked, half expecting him to tell her it was none of her business. It wasn't, but at this point, his business and hers were getting so intertwined that it was hard to tell where one left off and the other picked up.

"The painters can't finish my side until the end of the week. Somebody's daughter's getting married."

"That's what's got you into such a snit? A wedding?"

"The Jamisons have patched things up."

Several pieces of the puzzle came together. Jamison was the name of the couple who owned Driftwinds. Sasha didn't know anything about their personal lives, nor did she care, but evidently Jake was involved. "And that's bad?" she ventured after several minutes of silence. Fed, burped and dried, the baby slept soundly in the back seat. "If they're patching things up, where's the problem?"

It occurred to her to wonder if the peace negotiations would have any effect on her work at their cottage. Probably not, as she'd been hired by the rental agency, the only condition being that she finish the job before the holiday weekend began. It could do with a thorough airing and a couple of quarts of that spray the cleaning crew used to absorb odors, but other than that it was ready for occupancy.

"The problem," Jake said morosely, "is that I don't trust this truce. I accepted a retainer and I don't have a damn thing to show for it."

"What did you want to show for it?"

"Enough solid evidence so that he can't take her to the cleaners. Legally the place is joint property, but her money built it. All he's ever done is run for county office and lose. They keep wishy-washing around, but I'm not buying this reconciliation crap."

Sasha thought about it for several minutes. She thought briefly about her various divorces, but there was no comparison there. And then she thought about the man beside her, his muscular thighs sprawled out on the worn leather seat. *Laid-back* was the description that came to mind. Even when he was up to his ears in problems, he drove with a minimum of effort. None of this road rage you read about all the time.

She wondered if he did everything with the same minimum effort. "So what are you going to do, return the retainer?"

"I'm planning to. That's not what worries me." They were speaking quietly because of the sleeping baby in the back seat. "I have a feeling this won't be the end of it. Once we move your car away, Jamison might show up there for one last fling. I understand the place is booked solid all season after this week."

"Even if he's having an affair, why would he risk taking someone to his own cottage? That doesn't even make sense when there are all these hotels and motels around."

"It does if your face has been seen on as many campaign posters as his has. He'd be crazy to risk being seen sneaking into a motel with some bimbo."

She could think of a dozen arguments, but none worth voicing. Still, a detective had to start somewhere, and evidently Mrs. J. had reason to believe the cottage was the best bet. "Then you'll need me to baby-sit so you can take pictures." She added, "In case you get re-hired." And then tacked on, "If he's dumb enough to take some woman there, he deserves what he gets."

Jake continued to gnaw on his lower lip, obviously deep in thought. At least, she mused whimsically, he needed her for baby-sitting. She could build on that.

Build what? Woman, won't you ever learn?

Yes, but this is a two-fer.

Oh, shut up!

Granted, it didn't make a speck of sense for her to feel this bond with a baby she'd seen only hours ago—the grandchild of a man she'd known only a few days. While she might give the impression of being carefree and even somewhat superficial, by focusing on her career she had managed to ignore the ticking of her biological clock.

It had started ticking loud and clear the minute she had lifted a helpless infant into her arms.

"Look, we just passed the turn-off." Her conscience forced her to offer him an out. "If you drop me off at the cottage I can take Peaches and enough stuff to get by with home with me. Then you can hide out in the place next door and wait for something to happen. And this time," she added dryly, "you might want to be more careful about casting shadows and making noises."

He cut her a sidelong glance. "What, now you're giving me lessons in surveillance?"

"Well, I did catch you at it, remember?"

"Yeah, I remember." His mouth twisted in what was almost a smile.

She remembered, too. It was all part of that fate-engineered thing. After all these years, she had herself a baby. Albeit, a temporary one. "In case you were worried, you can take your time. On the Jamison thing, I mean—and anything else you need to do. I do a lot of my work at home, drawing up plans, ordering from suppliers." She didn't bother to mention taking in every yard sale, attic sale and estate sale within a day's drive of Muddy Landing. Those could wait. "I've got scads of stuff already on hand, so I won't need to go out anytime soon." Was she trying too hard to sell her services? Probably. She was powerfully attracted to the man, even though she'd known him less than a week—and he had a baby. And they needed her.

And maybe she needed to be needed.

"Thanks," he said dryly. Sasha tried and failed to read more into the single word. Then, without taking his eyes off the road—this close to Memorial Day weekend the midday traffic was dense and erratic—Jake laid a hand on her thigh. "How's the ankle?" he asked.

Her breath snagged in her throat. "I'd forgotten I had one." With his hand singeing a five-pointed brand on her thigh, she couldn't swear to having anything, especially a brain.

At the next stoplight, he turned to send her a wry grin. "Forgot you had an ankle? Believe me, I hadn't."

"Do I take that as a compliment?"

"Take it anyway you want." He reached across to brush the back of her neck, where her hair had long since escaped the decorative clips. "Why do you think I kept finding excuses to go back to your place? It's not exactly on the way to anywhere I need to be."

Her breath quickened. "I thought it was your guilty conscience." Not that he had any idea she'd been thinking about him when she'd tripped and fallen.

His fingers brushed her shoulder, then tucked a curl behind her ear. "Now why would I have a guilty conscience?" he teased. "I haven't done anything…yet."

Before she could come up with a halfway rational response, the car behind them honked impatiently. A stretch of several car lengths had opened up ahead of them since the light had turned green.

"Later," Jake growled, which did nothing at all to slow her heartbeat.

Was that a promise?

Or a threat?

Seven

Not until they pulled up in front of her house did either of them speak again. "Sasha, are you sure you want to do this?" Jake asked.

"I wouldn't have offered if there was the slightest doubt. If you'll just take in her bassinet and the rest of the stuff, we'll make out just fine, won't we, sugar dumpling?" Sasha unclipped her seatbelt and twisted around to check on their passenger. "Bless her heart, she's yawning—she looks just like a baby bird."

Jake took her keys and unloaded the car while Sasha counted baby toes and kissed both tiny feet. A few minutes later he returned. "You'll have to show me where you want stuff. Anything else you need, I can bring it tomorrow."

Tomorrow. Thinking of reasons to prolong the inevitable, she latched on to the promise. Sooner or later he'd come and claim his baby—the question was when? After he was done with the Jamison case, whichever way it turned out? Or maybe after his so-called interior decoration was complete? Who would she miss most, him or his baby?

Not even Solomon could answer that one, she thought ruefully.

"You sure you're up to this?" he asked, carefully unstrapping the seat and lifting seat and baby out.

Sasha led the way and held the door open. "Don't trip," she warned.

He gave her a look that defied interpretation. Placing baby, cradle and all on the coffee table, he turned to where she stood surrounded by an assortment of baby gear, plus her usual clutter. She forgot to breathe. Was it only her imagination that made her feel as if every cell in her body turned his way, like a sunflower following the sun?

Oh, Lord, she thought—all it took was the slightest encouragement and she was off on another fantasy, inventing a happy ending that wasn't going to happen.

"Sasha?" he said quietly. The house was suddenly so silent that even the quartz clock sounded loud.

"Mmm?" A complete mental and physical meltdown, that's all it was.

Jake placed his hands on her shoulders. It took only the slightest pressure to pull her into his arms. With her face against his hard, warm chest, she inhaled the scent that was pure Jake Smith. If his arms had fallen away she couldn't have moved. It was as if a giant magnet held her there.

"Fair warning. I'm about to kiss you," he said as calmly as if he were reading a public-service announcement.

In a voice that was only an octave or so higher than normal, she said, "Go ahead, I dare you."

He bit off a disbelieving laugh. She looked up, and then his face went out of focus and any hope of salvation fled from her mind.

Moist and surprisingly soft, Jake's mouth dragged against her lips, parting them. Beguiled by gentleness, she felt heat sparkle to life and flow through her veins like molten lava. Hunger was there, too, hovering in the background.

His control was maddening. Her hands fisted on the back of his shirt and she strained up onto her tiptoes. He was taller, but the three-inch soles of her sandals helped make up the difference.

And then he began to stroke her back, from shoulder to waist…and lower. When he cupped her hips to press her against his hardening groin, she wanted to tear off the layers between them.

He used his tongue. Not aggressively—not demandingly, but seductively, as if neither of them had anything better to do for the foreseeable future than to explore this thing that was happening between them.

This amazing thing that had been happening the very first time she'd ever laid eyes on him, even before she'd dialed 911, she admitted silently.

Ka-boom, ka-boom! The beat of her heart sounded like the jungle drums in those old Tarzan movies—or maybe it was his heart. The air around them was alive with electricity, she felt it all the way down to the soles of her feet.

By the time he lifted his face she was crushed in his arms so tightly she could hardly breathe. But then, who needed air? She rubbed her cheek against his shirt, inhaling his clean, sweaty scent. Please don't ever let me go, she begged silently. Let's just stay here like this for the next few years. Better yet, we could climb those stairs to where there's a queen-size bed, and—

A small sound made her catch her breath. "Peaches!" she gasped, pulling away at the thought of the small guest she had all but forgotten.

"Oh, honey—" She bent over to touch the fretful infant. "Let me take you out of that thing," she murmured.

"Wait a minute, I'll set up her bassinet." He sounded as calm as if he hadn't just kissed her senseless. "Where do you want it?"

"Oh, ah—upstairs, I guess. In my bedroom." She straightened up and glanced out the window. "Was that thunder?"

So maybe he wasn't responsible for all those special effects after all, she thought, chagrined. Only about ninety-seven percent of them.

Together they managed to get baby and bassinet upstairs. Sasha held her while Jake settled the wicker bed on a table, after clearing it of various items, including pictures of her family.

"What about sheets? Doesn't she need something on that pad?"

"Look in the hall. There's a linen closet. A pillowcase will do just fine until I unpack everything and wash the linens."

"The hall," he muttered, remaining where he was for a few moments.

Was he having trouble concentrating, too? Served him

right for opening a door she'd thought closed for good. She knew better than to build dreams on quicksand.

"How about bringing that rocking chair up from the living room?"

He finished slipping the bassinet pad into a mono-grammed Egyptian-cotton pillowcase. "You believe in rocking babies?"

She looked at him as if he'd lost his mind. "Why do you think the things were invented?"

"I remember we talked about getting one, but by the time we got around to it, Timmy was too big to be rocked." For a tough, sexy guy who could easily hold his own in almost any situation, he looked remarkably out of his element. "The one in the living room?"

"The one in the living room," she said softly, want-ing to hold him and his baby for the foreseeable future.

Jake placed the rocker in the only available space. "I'll get the rest of the stuff, then I'd better head back to Manteo." Not a word about the kiss they had shared, or about how long she could keep his baby—or when he'd be back.

Sasha knew when to leave well enough alone.

Jake brought up the three-drawer chest and several parcels, his masculine presence making waves in the de-cidedly feminine room. Fodder, she thought ruefully, for another round of erotic dreams.

Standing beside her bed, he looked down at his granddaughter. "You think she knows where she is?"

Sasha joined him there, standing close, but not touch-ing. "Of course she does. She's aware of color even if she can't see details. I'm positive she can feel the ambiance."

He slid his hands into his hip pockets. "The ambiance,

huh?" He glanced down at the antique Chinese rug in a faded shade of purple; at the ivory damask-patterned wallpaper and the green velvet fainting couch. Most of her furniture consisted of leftovers from various jobs or irresistibles from various estate sales. The fact that nothing went together didn't particularly bother her.

Smothering a smile, Sasha said, "You know what? I think she's far more intelligent than the average five-and-a-half-week-old." Boldly tucking her arm through his, she gazed at the solemn infant, knowing that she wouldn't be able to look at her lovely purple rug again without seeing a pair of size-twelve deck shoes planted firmly beside her queen-size bed.

What was that tacky old saying? He can park his shoes under my bed any old time?

She should be so lucky. Darn it, in spite of all her good intentions she'd gone and done it again. And now that he'd hooked and landed his baby-sitter, he was free to go about his business.

To give him credit, though, she was pretty sure that hadn't been his original intention. He'd been stunned at Timmy's call. What happened after that had simply happened, like a row of dominoes, each one tumbling the next.

"I know you have things to do," she murmured, hoping to hear him say he was in no hurry to leave.

He nodded, but made no move to go.

She tried to imprint him on her mind so that she could drag out the memory of him standing in the middle of her bedroom once he was no longer a part of her life. Probably not a good idea.

Searching for an impersonal topic to steer her away from temptation, she said, "I don't suppose the Jamison woman is your only client." According to Miss Martha, JBS Securities was seriously shorthanded. They had advertised, but so far, no one with the proper skills had applied.

"On top of that," the older woman had complained— if expressing a mild frustration could be called complaining—"Jake had to go and take on a private case."

All of which meant he was far too busy to deal with a grandchild, much less to get involved in a relationship. And while she might feel a powerful connection to him—that kiss alone had practically caused a brain meltdown—even if he was mildly interested in starting something, he didn't have time.

You buttered your bread, now lie in it, as Faylene would have said, and had on more than one occasion.

And she would. One more working mother. Working grandmother? One way or another she could do it.

The baby made a few experimental sounds and then let out a soft wail. Sasha shouldered Jake aside and said, "Here, give her to me. Come to mama, sugar pie. There, there, it's going to be all right, you wait and see." To Jake, she said, "Where did you put her bottles?"

"Come to *mama?*"

She curved a hand under the tiny body and supported her head. "Oh, hush, don't confuse her."

"Don't confuse yourself. And watch your step, will you? Those crazy shoes…" He frowned at her platform sandals.

Feeling vulnerable, Sasha promptly went on defense. "You do realize, don't you, that I've known this baby every bit as long as you have? My name is on her adoption papers, which gives me a personal interest. Besides, I'm obviously more experienced than you are." Holding the baby protectively, she glared at him.

"How do you figure that? Have you ever had a kid?"

"Twin sisters and a baby brother—I told you about them, remember? Chief baby-sitter and bottle washer. Not only that, next month I'm flying out to Oklahoma to be godmother to my best friend's first baby."

Was there such a thing as a god-grandmother?

"What are you planning to do with her? I mean, with my baby?"

"You mean right now? Tell you what—go downstairs and sit down in the living room and I'll let you hold her while I fix her a bottle."

Frowning, he appeared to consider her words. Hadn't he said the case he was working on was on hold? Sasha would be the first to admit she was being a bit presumptuous, but if she'd learned one thing, it was never to show weakness.

There was a casserole in the refrigerator that looked Mexican. Marty must have sent it by Faylene, so at least she wouldn't have to worry about supper. There was more than enough for two.

By the time she got back from the kitchen with a bottle of formula, Jake was tipped back in her ergonomic leather armchair with Peaches sprawled contentedly on his chest, gnawing on a tiny knuckle. "I think she's asleep," he whispered. "I'm afraid to move in case she starts crying again."

One more memory to tuck away in her album. Sasha stared just long enough to imprint the vision indelibly on her mind—the tough security man in the worn jeans and the faded black T-shirt, one big square hand covering practically the entire length of the tiny pink-clad infant.

"Things have changed a lot since I used to help Mama with the babies," she admitted as she lifted the limp form from his chest. "We actually used real diapers back then—the kind you wash and re-use. We didn't have a dryer, so in rainy weather we had drying diapers hanging all over the house. Most people were using disposables, but we couldn't afford them."

Way to go, gal! Like he really needed to know all that.

In case he'd forgotten them, she reminded him of the terrible twos, when toddlers went scouting for whatever trouble they could find—and found it. Double-trouble in the case of the twins, just about the time Buck came along. "Don't count on being able to concentrate until she's in kindergarten. By that time, if you're lucky, you should occasionally be able to get a few hours of work done."

She wondered how old Timmy had been when his mother had died, but couldn't think of a tactful way to ask. Holding the baby, she settled onto the sofa and touched her tiny lips with the nipple. When little Tuesday Smith took her cue and began suckling, she felt like crying because it felt so *right*.

Jake made no move to go. She probably should remind him of all the work he needed to be doing according to Miss Martha. Instead he was baby-sitting the baby-sitter.

Would he ever kiss her again? Could she go on living if he didn't?

Talk about going on a diet.

His long legs were crossed at the ankles, his arms

crossed over his chest. His eyes were narrowed, but not quite closed. He looked comfortable. Comfortable, tired and beautiful in the way certain men could look beautiful, that had nothing to do with any particular arrangement of features.

She thought of all the unhandsome Hollywood heroes she'd seen in movies and fallen in love with. Robert Mitchum and James Coburn. Charles Bronson and that guy who used to race around on a motorcycle—Steve McQueen. It all boiled down to chemistry. Like an elusive perfume that was impossible to describe. Either a woman reacted to it or it left her cold.

Nothing about the man seated across the room left her cold. That was something she was going to have to deal with—the sooner, the better. "What colors are you painting your house?" she asked, testing to see if he'd fallen asleep. It was drizzling outside, but not all that late, even though it seemed as if a week had passed since she'd first woken up that morning.

"Hmm?" He blinked his eyes. They widened, darkened and then narrowed as he glanced at his watch. "White."

"I mean the other side, where you live." The outside of the entire building was white. The office, which was all she'd seen, was white. She could have suggested something with a little more pizzazz if she'd been asked. For a security firm, maybe sand with caramel accents and small shots of navy and teal—something solid, reassuring and masculine.

"What about it?" he asked querulously. At least he was awake now.

"What colors are you using?"

"I told you—white." His chest rose and fell. His hands were still laced across the broad expanse. She wanted to be his hands. The plain, embarrassing truth was, she wanted to be all over him, inside and out. Maybe one desperate last fling?

Have you no pride?

Nope. Not a smidge.

From the chair, which was more comfortable than it looked, Jake watched through half-closed eyes. She was a natural. Those hips, the curve of her arms that was just right to hold a baby. Her breasts…. She probably thought she needed to lose a few pounds, but to his way of thinking she was perfect just as she was. Built just the way a woman should be built.

Cut it out, man. This is exactly the kind of thinking that got you in trouble back in high school. The same kind that landed your son in trouble ten months ago.

At least he'd married the mother of his kid. He had a feeling Tim and Cheryl were better off not going that far, but who was to say? Things were what things were.

Great. Now he was waxing philosophical. If he needed a clue that it was time to go, that was it. This baby was his responsibility, not hers, but Jake didn't kid himself that his granddaughter was the sole problem.

A large part of the problem was Sasha. It had been a long time since any woman had affected him the way she did. Hell, he'd been half aroused ever since he'd seen her sprawled out on the Jamisons' upper deck, with her shirt plastered to her breasts and her shapely legs sprawled out like an invitation. She was nothing at all like Rosemary.

Abruptly, he got to his feet. "I'd better hit the road, it's getting late."

She didn't say a word. Her eyes said everything for her, although he couldn't have interpreted the message if his life depended on it. Didn't she want him to go and leave her alone with his baby? To stay? What? Hell, he didn't even know for sure what color her eyes were.

Peaches was fed, clean, dry and sound asleep again when Marty's white van pulled up in front of the house and two women piled out. When Marty had called half an hour ago about the fund-raiser, Sasha had told her about the baby and all that had happened over the past several hours.

"Shh, y'all be quiet, I just got her down," she whispered by way of greeting.

"I can't believe it, you've got a baby!" Marty squealed. "I've got to see her. Wait'll I tell Daisy!"

The three women tiptoed upstairs to the bedroom. "Oh-h, she's so tiny," Marty whispered.

"Now you done stepped in it," was Faylene's only comment, but her voice was noticeably lacking its usual astringency.

"Come on down to the kitchen." Sasha led the way, hardly limping at all.

"I see you're getting around better. I brought you another casserole when I came by earlier on my way to the post office. Good thing I left out the jalapeños. Nursing mothers, you know." Marty snickered.

Faylene got right to the point. "We've thought up the perfect way to get Lily and this security fellow together. Things are gonna be closed up tighter'n a tick for the holiday, so he won't be working. This big do at the community center on Monday, they got the school band from over to the college in Elizabeth City comin' to play, and lemme tell you, they're *good!*"

"I'm not taking this baby around all those people," Sasha said flatly.

"Who said anything about you and her going? Lily's gonna be there helping out with the donations, so all you need to do is get this Smith fellow to carry whatever you're fixin' to donate over there for you."

"I told you, Jake lives in Manteo."

"So? He'll be coming here to see his baby, won't he?" Faylene blinked her eyes, the effect dramatic. She was the only woman in their small circle who wore more makeup than Sasha did.

"If she's still here," Sasha cautioned. "I'm only keeping her until his paint fumes are gone and the roofers finish hammering."

"You'll think of something," Marty said. "Tell him she's got the sniffles and it'll be weeks before she can be around fresh paint, then tell him you need something carried over to the center and can he come take it for you so you won't have to take her around all those crowds."

"You two are awful! That's the weakest plot I've ever heard!"

Marty picked up the book Sasha had been reading over breakfast only this morning. My God, when had her life taken such a bizarre turn? "What'd you think of her latest one?" the bookseller asked, holding up the paperback novel by one of the top romantic suspense writers.

"Speaking of weak plots?" Sasha retorted. "All right,

so maybe he'll let me keep her a few more days, but I can't ask him to take anything—and by the way, what *is* my contribution? I haven't even had time to think, I've been so busy."

"Go through all that flea-market junk you got laying around," the housekeeper said. "You got a whole herd of white elephants you need to chase outta here so I can clean this place."

Sasha had to laugh. It was true. She happened to have a weakness for used personal treasures of past generations, partly because she had nothing at all from her own family, partly because just one such item placed in the right setting could change the focus of an entire room.

"Okay, so *if* she's still here over the weekend, and *if* Jake happens to show up, and *if* he'll agree to run an errand for me, I'll send him over there with that alabaster lamp or maybe that brass sconce I haven't been able to place. He'll spot Lily, fall madly in love and swoon at her feet, is that your plan?"

Marty nibbled on a crust from the casserole she'd brought over earlier. Frowning, she murmured, "Not enough cheese."

"Next time use processed cheese slices, like I told you," said Faylene, the uncontested world's worst cook. "Look, we got her lined up to list stuff as it comes in with folks' names for them that wants something off on their taxes. Who better'n her to know the rules?"

"Monday noon's the deadline," Marty warned, "so you need to get him over there before then."

Sasha poured three glasses of sweet tea and led the way into the living room. If they stayed in the kitchen long enough, Marty would taste up every bit of the food she'd brought. Marriage seemed to have increased her appetite. "All right, let's say I can get him over here. Let's say I can prevail on him to take my donation over to the community center and say he sees Lily. What happens then? He proposes, she accepts and bingo, another match is made? Y'all are getting giddy. You know, we used to be better at this."

"And we used to have more to work with." Marty sighed. "That's the part we haven't thought out yet, but we're working on it. Lily's lost a few pounds she can't really spare, but she's still the most beautiful woman in town, present company excepted, of course."

"Of course," Sasha said dryly, and tossed today's paper at her. It was still bagged in a plastic sleeve.

Marty said, "You read the ads yet? You going to Norfolk Monday for the big sales?"

"I thought I was supposed to stay here with the baby and set up your pigeon."

"Oh, yeah. Why do they always plan everything for the same day?"

"Because it's the holiday, you goose."

They all laughed. Faylene washed the few dishes in the sink and then the two women left, offering to pick up any groceries she needed now that she wasn't quite so mobile.

Sasha closed the door and leaned against it, picturing the elegant accountant they'd been discussing. Over my dead body, she thought.

Beneath a rapidly darkening sky, a narrow band of pink sliced across the horizon as Jake drove home, his thoughts touching on his granddaughter, his son, the on-again-off-again Jamisons and the sexy, maddening woman he'd just left.

Sasha Lasiter, alias Sally June Parrish and evidently several other names. Was anything about her genuine?

Did he care?

Yeah, he cared. Not for his own sake, but for his baby's. Was he crazy to leave his granddaughter with a woman he'd known for less than a week?

The trouble was, she felt like someone he'd known all his life—and would like to know a whole lot better. So far as he knew, she hadn't tried to hide anything about her past. A superficial check of public records had pretty well corroborated what she'd told him—not that he'd expected any surprises.

Sally June Parrish, born September 28, 1967, married Lawrence Combs, married Barry Cassidy, married Russell Boone, married Frank Lasiter, with divorces spaced at suitable intervals.

She admitted freely to dyed hair, tinted contacts and fake fingernails and eyelashes. So what about her was genuine?

Admittedly, not much. Only the things that mattered, like her heart, her character—that self-deprecating sense of humor that knocked out his defenses.

One of the things he'd uncovered was the fact that she'd been doing pro bono work for years at various women's shelters and nursing homes. She was a regular speaker for various girls' groups. God knows what she taught them—how to make the most of their physical assets? How to throw together a roomful of mismatched furniture and make it come out looking pretty good? How to laugh even when you catch a heel in a crack and damn near break a leg?

None of that, he admitted as he headed home, explained the crazy way she affected him. The way she'd affected him right from the start, when he'd been shooting pictures of a lush-looking redhead sprawled out on Jamison's deck, soaking up sun while she waited for her lover to arrive.

At least that's what he'd thought at the time. Even then he'd envied Jamison without ever having met the guy. The lady would have tempted any man, married or not.

It had been a long time since Jake had looked at a woman that way. Okay, so maybe he'd looked—hell, he wasn't over the hill, far from it—but it had been a while since he'd been tempted to do anything about it. Raising a son, plus operating a business, had taken all his time and most of his energy after Rosemary had died when Timmy was seven.

Sure, he'd gone out with a few women. Dinner and a movie, that sort of thing. He'd even gone dancing at one of the nightclubs out on the beach a few times, but none of the women he'd dated turned him on. Not that they weren't attractive, but under the sleek tans, the tight jeans and the shaggy bleached hair, they'd been pretty much cut from the same pattern. Mostly they talked about movies he hadn't seen, celebrities he'd never heard of, reality shows he'd been too busy with real life to bother watching.

Sasha, on the other hand, set her own style. She definitely wasn't built to today's standards. Her clothes, even when she was supposed to be working, were neither beachy nor practical, yet he couldn't imagine her in a tailored dress or a two-piece business suit. From her crazy shoes to the top of her tousled red hair, she was the kind of woman all men dreamed of taking to bed.

Which meant she probably had men stacked up like cordwood, waiting for her to return their calls.

Reluctantly turning off the semierotic daydream, he parked in the backyard, leaving the three-car space out front available to any drop-in customers. With the holiday weekend bearing down fast—it looked to be a rainy one, too, which was never a good sign—there'd be a bunch of false alarms and screw-ups as cottages filled up with people who didn't take time to read a simple set of instructions.

He went in through the back door, frowning at the smell of paint. Work would stop for the holiday. It was a wonder they'd even got this far. Once the job was finished he could air out the rooms and bring his granddaughter home where she belonged.

Yeah? And what about the woman? Where does she belong?

He knew where he wanted her, all right. In his bed, now and for the foreseeable future, or at least until he ran out of steam and his boilers shut down.

And that made about as much sense as anything else in this cosmic comedy he called his life. Starting with that call from Timmy, his modestly rewarding, occasionally interesting, but mostly predictable life had changed beyond all recognition.

He couldn't imagine Rosemary, who'd been only twenty-six years old when she'd died, as a grandmother. She'd been a good mother—casual, but just what a boy needed, especially once he started getting interested in sports. She'd never been much for rocking or cuddling, but that was just her style.

Sasha, on the other hand...

Yeah, well...this was a whole new ball game. If there was a rule book for this kind of situation, he'd better find it and do some fast cramming, because the game had already started.

Passing through his freshly painted, semifurnished living room on his way to the shower, he wondered if tonight was too soon to drive back to Muddy Landing. Traffic died down after dark—he could make it in less than forty-five minutes.

On the other hand, if he put in a couple of hours in the office, he'd be good to go first thing tomorrow.

By the time he stepped under the needle spray, he was whistling under his breath. It wasn't a lullaby.

Eight

Was that the phone? At the shrill sound, the dream that had started out as wishful fantasy and morphed into something wildly erotic shattered and began to fade. Desperately, Sasha sought to hold on, but the bits and pieces slipped away like handfuls of fog.

She was on the upper deck of an oceanfront cottage in a canopied bed, and she was not alone—there was someone in bed with her, someone who was...

Gone.

A few glimpses lingered then disappeared. The feelings they engendered lingered longest of all, but in the end there was nothing left but a wisp of memory and a nagging sense of dissatisfaction.

Reluctantly, she opened her eyes. She was in her own living room, not on the upper deck of a half-familiar oceanfront cottage—lying on her own linen-slipcovered sofa instead of a canopied bed. Even more depressing, she was alone. She remembered putting the baby in her bassinet and coming back downstairs to turn out the lights and lock up for the night. She'd decided to read a few pages....

The shrill sound came again. It was the doorbell, not the phone. And the background noise was rain drumming down on the roof, not the ocean swishing against the shore.

"Oh, for Pete's sake, hang on, I'm coming, I'm coming," she muttered. Squinting against the glare of a reading lamp and the hall fixture, she hobbled to the door to see who on earth was calling at this hour. Middle-of-the-night visitors always meant trouble. She wished now she'd had a peephole installed in her front door, but it wouldn't have fit with her seasonal wreaths.

With her hand on the doorknob she blinked at her watch and waited for her eyes to focus. Seven minutes before *ten?* Oh, for heaven's sake, she hadn't slept more than twenty minutes at most. It only seemed longer because of that crazy dream.

She opened the door and there he stood. Her crazy dream in person. Wet hair falling over his forehead, rain glistening on the shoulders of a navy windbreaker bearing the logo of the North Carolina Aquarium on Roanoke Island.

They spoke at the same time. She said, "What do you want?"

He said, "I brought some stuff we forgot. I meant to wait until morning, but—"

Turning him away wasn't an option. Besides, he had no way of knowing she'd just been dreaming about him. Unless...

No, that was crazy.

"Come on in...I guess." He was probably worried about his baby. While he was here she could talk to him about attending the fund-raiser. "What's that?" She blinked at the red nylon bundle under his arm.

"It's, a—a backpack, I guess you'd call it. You put a baby in it and carry it on your back while you shop or run or do whatever else you need to do." He shook it out, holding it by the shoulder straps.

"While I *run?*"

"Yeah, well...some people do."

"Do I look like a runner to you?" She stepped back and led the way into the living room before she remembered that before her nap she had showered, toweled her hair and left it to air-dry, giving forty-seven cowlicks their freedom. She had slathered on moisturizer, eye cream and lip balm, and she was wearing her favorite at-home costume.

This is not about me, she told herself, it's about the baby. "Did you carry Timmy around in a sack on your back when he was barely six weeks old?" Feeling challenged always put her on the offensive. "That's scary."

He didn't react the way he was supposed to. Instead, he looked bemused. With a half smile on his face, his eyes moved slowly from her bare feet to her naked freckles, to her wild, slept-in hair.

"We had a baby carriage. Rosemary used to wheel him all over town. After supper, we both took him for carriage rides. Later on it was wagon rides, tricycle rides, bicycle rides without the training wheels."

"Yes, well, Peaches is too small for a backpack, and in case you failed to notice, sidewalks are rare in my neighborhood."

"I think you can wear it in front, too. That'd work, wouldn't it?"

Wear what—the sidewalk? With her brain out on disability, she quickly changed the subject. "You're dripping. No matter how much you water them those flowers aren't going to grow any bigger." She pointed to the stylized blossoms in her faded Oriental rug.

"You want me to leave?" He sounded plaintive, and she was pretty sure it was deliberate. A splendid specimen of prime masculinity, and he sounded *plaintive?*

I don't think so, Sasha thought, amused in spite of her irritation. Amused because he had a way of doing that to her. Irritated because he'd caught her looking her unadorned worst. The heroine of her X-rated dream hadn't been any freckled, overweight woman wearing a fright wig.

She smoothed her hair back from her face and did her instant face-lift, raising her brows, tilting her chin and sucking in her cheeks. It was one of the first things Sally June Parrish, with all her insecurities, had taught herself to do. She'd practiced for hours in front of a cracked and speckled mirror.

"Could I see her?" Jake whispered.

"She's asleep."

"I won't wake her, I just want to look at her again."

Sasha knew how he felt. How many times had she tiptoed upstairs to the bedroom just to make sure she hadn't imagined the whole thing?

"All right, but leave that thing in the foyer. I hope you saved the receipts."

"What's the difference between a foyer and a hall?"

At the foot of the stairs, she shook her head. "Don't

try to change the subject, I'm not having this conversation with you. You want to see Peaches, come on. Two minutes, that's all. Infants need all the undisturbed sleep they can get and this one has already been through enough of an upheaval."

Once more they stood side by side, close enough so that she caught a hint of soap and aftershave and something that was uniquely healthy male. Uniquely Jake.

She could feel his body heat as together they gazed down at the sleeping infant.

Jake whispered. "God, she's little, isn't she?"

"Shh. What did you expect, that she'd grown in the last few hours?"

"I think Timmy was bigger at that age, but it's been a long time."

He was standing so close his breath stirred her hair against her cheek. She did her best to ignore the tickling sensation. If he noticed her irregular breathing she could blame it on the stairs. It was no big secret that she was hardly the athletic type. "Boys are born bigger."

She knew better than that, it just popped out. Her father had called Buck the runt of the litter, among a few less-flattering things.

"Her hair looks like it's going to be curly. Tim had curls when he was born."

His warm, coffee-scented breath on her cheek raised a flurry of goose bumps along her flank. "That's not hair, it's peach fuzz."

He smiled, and then she did. As several minutes ticked past, Jake made no move to leave. Neither did Sasha. Even though the bedroom smelled of Odalisque perfume and baby powder, she was far more aware of the clean, earthy scent of his body that the rain had only accentuated. The only light in the room came from a pink-shaded lamp with a bronze Venus-on-the-halfshell body—another of her flea-market finds.

Suddenly the intimacy was smothering. Jake took a deep breath and expelled it in an uneven sigh. "Trust me, it'll grow out curly."

She didn't dare trust him, but she wasn't about to argue. The sooner he left, the less likely she'd be tempted to do something incredibly stupid. It wouldn't be the first time, but she had a feeling that this time the effects would be far more lasting.

Tucking her arm through his, she steered him out into the hall. "That's four minutes. You've used up your viewing allotment for the next two days."

"No way. Don't forget whose baby she is."

She smirked. "Don't forget who can't take care of her because he's in the middle of having his house painted in colors I wouldn't use on an outdoor privy."

"What the hell do my colors have to do with anything? Besides, last I heard white wasn't even a color."

"Shh, keep your voice down," she hissed as she flounced down the stairs. Pride was a marvelous analgesic. Her ankle didn't hurt at all.

Jake followed two steps behind, his feet thudding solidly on the carpeted stairs. At the foot of the stairs she spun around, but before she could say a word he clamped his hands on her shoulders and leaned over until his face was on a level with hers. "Listen to me. Just because I'm allowing you to keep her for a few days, you don't want to lose sight of who she belongs to."

Her gaze strayed from his narrowed eyes to his lips. Big mistake.

"The minute the work crew clears out I intend to hook up an exhaust fan and pump the place out so by the time I get her back where she belongs, you won't be able to smell a thing but good, fresh air."

"Ha!" she said weakly. With his hands gripping her shoulders and his face only inches away from hers, it was the best she could do.

"Damn right, *ha!* This has been one hell of a day, in case you hadn't noticed. I've spent most of it on the highway going back and forth between your place, my place, Cheryl's and the lawyer's, not to mention all that shopping. On the way here tonight I ran out of gas, and on top of that, the barbecue place was closed, so I haven't had anything to eat since lunch—and in case you forgot, I didn't get to finish that."

She started to interrupt but he cut her off. "Look, I'm not the sweetest guy you ever met, even when I'm in a good mood. When I'm tired, ticked off and hungry that goes double. So don't mess with me, lady, because I'm not in the mood to play games."

Somewhere during the tirade Sasha's mouth had fallen open. Her eyes had widened, while his had gone from warm hazel to cold obsidian. It was several moments before she noticed that his fingers were no longer biting into her shoulders, but had moved to the bare skin above the boat-necked caftan. "Sasha?" He sounded almost puzzled.

Unable to look away, she murmured, "Hmm?"

"I don't know what you're doing to me, but…"

And then he closed the few inches between them.

The instant before his face went out of focus, she saw his mouth soften. Then his lips brushed hers, pressed lightly and lifted before she could come to her senses enough to react.

Desperate to reclaim his touch, she took the initiative. Standing on tiptoe, she kissed him, using the tip of her tongue to lure him into responding.

By the time the kiss ended they were on the sofa with no memory of having moved. Jake's hands had found their way under her voluminous caftan. She wore panties underneath—just barely. As she wasn't wearing a bra, there was nothing to impede the way of a pair of determined hands.

He settled over her, covering half her body. There was a baby in her bedroom, otherwise she'd have led him right back upstairs.

"Talk about going from zero to sixty in ten seconds flat," he said with a short laugh.

"I know of a Lamborghini that does it in four," she replied, her voice no steadier than his.

"Sorry. Six-year-old Suburban. Ten's my best finish."

"Are we—?" Finished, she meant. Her faded caftan was up around her shoulders, her body fully revealed, flaws and all. She had managed to tug his shirt from his belt so that she could run her hands over his muscular torso. Discovering his sensitive areas, she concentrated on those, thrilling to the way he gasped when she brushed his nipples. Her fingers trailed down to his belt buckle and he sucked his breath audibly.

With a catch in his voice, Jake said, "Finished? I hope not. I don't suppose this couch of yours opens up?"

"No, but there's a downstairs bedroom."

"I can probably make it that far."

Sasha wasn't at all sure she could even stand. For the first time she regretted being a collector. There was no room to spread out where they were. He wouldn't be able to straighten his legs without kicking over a stack of something.

He stood and pulled her to her feet and into his arms. Sasha couldn't remember the last time she'd wanted a man as much as she wanted this one. The year she'd discovered sex, it had been more a matter of adolescent hormones than anything else. Comparing what she'd felt then to what she was feeling now was like comparing wading in a plastic pool to diving off the continental shelf. Both involved getting wet, but one involved testing unexplored depths.

"Which way?" he asked, his voice barely audible.

"That way," she replied without moving away. His exploring hands cupped her breasts and her knees threatened to buckle. Wrapping her arms around his waist, she held on to his belt. When her fingers slipped inside his jeans she was glad that for once she wasn't impeded by her usual array of rings. His hips felt as hard as they looked. He was hard everywhere—hard and sweet and utterly intoxicating.

With only a few more hungry kisses along the way they managed to make it to the spare room. At the moment it looked more like a warehouse than a bedroom, but at least the bed was relatively uncluttered.

Sasha swept away a stack of fabric samples and several catalogs while Jake dug his wallet out of his hip pocket, withdrew a foil packet and placed it on the bedside table.

She started to lie down, and then hesitated. Undress first? Wait to see if he wanted to undress her? Race to see who could get naked first and dive into bed together?

For a woman who'd been married four times, she suddenly felt as awkward as a virgin bride. What if he didn't like her? What if he thought she was too fat? She had a few stretch marks. She thought of them as damask, but Jake probably didn't even know what damask was.

She was still dithering when Jake lifted the caftan over her head and tossed it at the chair. Tomorrow she would tear the wretched thing into dust rags—or maybe press it in her memory book.

"Last chance to back out," he said.

As if backing out was even a faint possibility.

Quickly, he stripped off his shirt, stepped out of his shoes and shed jeans and briefs in one smooth motion, his eyes never leaving her face. She tried not to stare, but oh my, he was...

The word *glorious* came to mind, but even that didn't do him justice. Turning away, she folded back the bedspread. She hadn't even been sure there were sheets on the bed, not that it would have mattered.

He slid her yellow bikini panties down her hips, then lowered her onto the bed and came down beside her, burying his face in her throat. His tongue stroked her pulse until she wanted to scream at him. Her thighs moved restlessly. She wanted him inside her to end this exquisite torture, yet she didn't want it to end—this desperate compulsive tension that was building, aching, throbbing inside her.

The scent of arousal eddied around them as she felt him thrust involuntarily against her belly. Moisture blossomed as her eager body prepared the way. When he drew the lobe of her ear into his mouth, she groaned. When his lips moved down her throat to her breast to suckle there, she soared to a higher level, desperately near the edge.

When he moved his attentions to her other breast, circling her nipple with his tongue, her feet arched and her thighs fell apart.

This was her dream. *This* was what her dream had been all about!

Weak from all the attention lavished on long-neglected places, she caught a shuddering breath, then gasped for breath again as he took her even closer to the edge of the chasm. Her mind flickered in and out as his kisses and his clever hands wove a magic spell on her body.

If this was a dream, let it never end. Awake or asleep, he was all her fantasies come alive.

He whispered something, the words muffled against her throat. He nipped the underside of her chin with tender, ferocious kisses, then moved on to nibble her cheeks, her lips, as if he couldn't get enough of her taste. His palm stroked her belly, his fingertips tracing the creases of her groin before feathering lightly across her mound.

When his fingers slipped inside her, his thumb stroking her until she was ready to scream, she could only whimper. Torn between wanting to prolong the exquisite agony and the desperate need to end it, she cried softly, "Please…"

"Shh, sweetheart, we're getting there, give me a minute…"

When he sat up and leaned away, she thought she

would die. Don't bother with that thing, she wanted to scream at him.

So much for intelligence. So much for survival skills.

And then she stopped thinking at all as he moved over her again. In a jumble of limbs, her toes pushed against the tops of his feet, her knees bumped against his, and he knelt over her, her thighs embracing his hips. Her hands moved restlessly over the parts of him she could reach. She'd thought she was experienced? Nothing even faintly resembling this had happened to her before—this intensity that made every cell in her body quiver in anticipation.

Just then, lightning brightened the room. A moment later thunder rumbled across the sky. It seemed appropriate considering the electricity they were generating inside.

Jake took her hands and moved them slowly down his body, lingering where he wanted her attention. She gave it eagerly, testing his powers of resistance against her own power to arouse, first with feathery fingertip caresses, then with the judicious use of her fingernails.

First thing tomorrow, the acrylic goes.

Finally wrenching her hands away, he gently thrust inside her, withdrew and then thrust again. She whimpered, moving her hips restlessly. Hurry, hurry, hurry!

"What are you trying to do, woman—cripple me for life?"

"Am I succeeding?" she panted hopefully.

"Slow down, slow down—short fuse."

When she felt him withdraw she tried to grasp his shoulders, but her hands slipped off his sweat-slick skin. Then he turned, levered himself to a sitting position, and with his back braced against the padded headboard, lifted her astride his lap.

"Oh, yesss," she breathed as she wriggled against his groin. In the dim light from a small table lamp, his strained features could have been chiseled from stone.

His eyes were closed, his head back. He moved with carefully measured thrusts, his breath coming in raw gasps. "Sure you're not registered somewhere—as a—lethal agent?" he ground out.

And then there was no more room for words. Suddenly she was clinging to him, desperately trying to match the furious pace of his thrusts as fireworks began to burst around her, exploding in a brilliance of pulsating color. As if from a distance she heard a guttural cry and then her own voice cascaded over her in a series of soft, wild whimpers.

Breathless, she collapsed against his sweat-damp chest. His head was back against the headboard, his eyes still closed, his hands still gripping her hips.

Once she was able to think again, her first thought was not for herself, but for the infant upstairs. Any moment now she would need to be fed again. It had been so long since she'd cared for a baby that she'd almost forgotten what a full-time job it was. And as inevitable as it seemed, this thing that was happening between her and Jake vastly complicated an already complex situation.

They should have laid out the ground rules first.

Like what? No messing around until she's a year old? Two years old?

Where would Jake be by that time? Where would Jake's grandchild be?

Chances were, neither of them would be upstairs in her bedroom.

Nine

Sex had to be the world's best cure for insomnia, Sasha thought sometime later as she stretched luxuriantly. Parts of her body were so deliciously tender that she was half aroused just remembering. Slowly, she opened her eyes and realized it was morning, and she was still in the spare bed instead of her own upstairs bedroom.

Who had fed the baby?

There was no sign of Jake, but someone had pulled the top sheet up over her shoulders. It probably wasn't the tooth fairy.

Her first thought was Peaches. As long as she'd been delegated baby-sitter-in-chief, she intended to do a first-class job of it. Whatever happened once Jake reclaimed his granddaughter, he'd have no room for complaint on that score.

As for anything else…

Time would tell. She had the world's worst taste in picking husbands, but then, in this case, no one had mentioned marriage.

Upstairs, she looked in on the baby, marveling that anything so precious, so perfect, was sharing her bedroom, even temporarily. But then, her house didn't reek of paint and varnish. Nobody was crawling around on her roof, sounding like a cavalry brigade.

She even had a few dependable friends who would gladly take over if she had to be away for a few hours. How many available women friends did Jake have?

Well. It was a tad late to be wondering about Jake's women.

There was a half-empty bottle on the dressing table. Evidently Jake had fed her before he'd left. She collected the bottle and tiptoed away. Changing could wait. Sleep was important at this age.

What else was important? It had been so long. She remembered from back when Annie, Jeannie and Buck had been babies, when first one, and then the other two, would reach the five-alarm stage, loosely interpreted as, "I want it, and I want it *now!*"

It had taken Sasha and her mother together just to handle the twins. By the time Buck came along, Sasha knew the drill. She'd had almost complete care of the new baby while their mother tried to tame the unmanageable twins.

A few years later the three youngest members of the Parrish clan had closed ranks. She could still see them exploding from the school bus, racing up the path to the house, laughing, chattering, the girls finishing each other's sentences. Buck had been the pesky, tagalong brother, but even so, the three of them had enjoyed a closeness that had excluded her. As baby-sitter-in-chief, she'd ranked along with their parents as an authority figure—someone to be obeyed when absolutely necessary, but never included, much less confided in. At the time, she hadn't particularly resented it, but later, after she'd left home, it had made her feel sad.

Of course, Buck was gone now, but she and her sisters chatted on the phone whenever she called. They sent pictures of their families when she asked for them, which she framed and set around her house, if only to remind her that she did have a family. Their Christmas cards always included family newsletters all about promotions and camping trips and school honors, and she tried to feel a part of it all, but there was no real closeness involved. There never had been.

Maybe she should do a family newsletter. Hey, y'all, I've finally got a baby. She's only on loan, but then, I'm really too busy with all my commissions to have her full-time, anyway. Oh, and by the way, I'm in love again, and this time I have a feeling it's terminal. Ha-ha.

Ten minutes later when she tiptoed into the room again she was met by a pair of unblinking eyes in a red, tear-wet face. "Oh, honey pie, don't do that," she murmured, trying to remember the words of a lullaby she used to sing to the twins. She hummed and la-la-ed while she did the necessary cleaning and changing. Those solemn blue eyes followed her every move.

"What are you thinking, dumpling? You're not sure you like all this roadrunning you've been doing lately? You're missing your granddaddy?" She swallowed a laugh. "Oh, honey, so am I," she whispered, lifting the baby to her shoulder. "So am I."

So am I...

The first thing Jake had done on his way home was to arrange to have the Lexus picked up and driven to Muddy Landing. He dropped off the keys at a garage— the owner owed him a couple of favors—and drove the rest of way thinking about the next item on the agenda.

Next item, hell. All he wanted to do was turn back, crawl into her bed and stay there for the foreseeable future.

But if the first four guys she married couldn't satisfy her, what gave him the idea she'd be interested in an over-the-hill widower?

Maybe not over the hill—he'd pretty well proved he was still good for a few rounds—still, he was a meat-and-potatoes type and she was definitely caviar.

First stop, the office. Jake checked his phone messages while he scanned the note Miss Martha had left for him saying that she wouldn't be in until eleven or thereabouts. It was early yet for Hack. Feeling restless and vaguely unsettled, he started going through his schedule for the following week. Two installations, which he enjoyed. Three repairs, which he didn't. There was still the Jamison thing. He'd been called off, but something still didn't feel right.

In the middle of checking the addresses of the repair jobs, he paused. God, I've got a baby!

Allowing Sasha to get involved had been a mistake, but short of driving her back to Kitty Hawk and dumping her out at her car, at what point could he have excluded her? From start to finish, it had gone down like a row of dominoes.

She was right about one thing, he thought, unlocking the inside door that separated his private office from his living quarters. This was no place to bring a kid. The office was gradually airing out, but his side stunk to high heaven.

Hands on his hips, he looked around, trying to see his familiar living quarters objectively. What the devil had she meant when she'd criticized his color scheme? What was wrong with white walls, white ceilings and brown floors? Not everybody wanted to live in a lavender house with green trim, filled with the kind of furniture a guy couldn't even pronounce.

Shedding his clothes along the way, he headed for the shower, which was also painted white. What the hell had he been thinking about, getting mixed up with a woman like Sasha Lasiter?

Answer: he hadn't been thinking, at least not with his brain.

A short while later, showered, shaved and dressed in a clean version of the jeans and T-shirt he'd discarded, Jake was already outside when the office phone rang. He grabbed it on the fourth ring. "JBS Security, Jake Smith."

And then, "Mrs. Jamison?"

Several minutes later he replaced the phone. If he were inclined to be superstitious he might blame it on the phase of the moon, or some weird conjunction of planets. First Sasha, then the baby, then Sasha again— in a big way—and now this crazy on-again, off-again case he'd been working on when it had all started.

Evidently it was now on again. According to his wife, Jamison had lulled her into calling off the dogs, but the minute she lowered her guard, he'd cut the connubial cord. According to his wife, the guy had the morals of a rat snake. She wanted the goods on him, and she wanted it yesterday.

The lady didn't need a private investigator as much as she needed a sharp lawyer. Something here stunk to high heaven. Jake couldn't put his finger on it, and without evidence there wasn't a lot he could do. Trouble was, it was probably already too late.

But as long as he was back on retainer, Jake figured he might as well continue to stake out the cottage again, as Mrs. J. seemed convinced that that was where he was taking his girlfriend. During the time he'd spent watching the place, he had seen no evidence of it, other than a certain sexy redhead making herself at home on the upper deck.

Meanwhile, Hack could do the usual check, see if he could pick up another lead. Jamison was a local, his wife was from Virginia Beach. They owned properties in both places, and with the state line so close, things could get complicated.

Before he left the office, he made another attempt to reach his son. He'd tried several times in the past few hours, leaving a message each time. This time he connected on the first try.

"Hey, Dad, I was just about to call you. Jeez, I've been going crazy, wondering what was going down. Have you seen her yet? Is everything all right? Is Cheryl gonna let you have her?"

"Whoa, back up—first, everything's fine here.

Cheryl seemed relieved to let her go to family—I told her she can see the baby anytime she wants to. I've been thinking, though—did you ask Cheryl about her folks? I mean, genetically, it might be a good idea to know something about her background. I tried to get some information from her, but the way things went down, it was a pretty emotional time for all of us."

"I know her mom's dead. She and her old man don't get along. I think he drinks a lot or something. Anyway, I don't know all that much about her folks, but Cheryl's a nice girl. What do you think, is the baby okay?"

"Ah, son—she's a real beauty." Jake saw no reason to mention that she was bald and had a voice like a fire siren when she really cut loose. "All her working parts appear to be in good order, especially her lungs. I cleaned her up and gave her a bottle earlier this morning, and left her sleeping like a baby."

"You *left* her? Left her *where?*"

"Whoa, no cause for panic." So then he had to explain about Sasha and how she'd been caught up in the whole procedure, and how she'd agreed to keep the baby until the roofers were finished and he could get rid of the paint fumes. "You'd like her, son. She's good with babies—in fact, she's the one who got us in to see a lawyer so we could sew up things in record time."

"Okay…I guess. I mean, I trust your judgment, Dad, but Cheryl, is she okay with this?"

"She's fine." He could explain in more detail later. "Everything went down without a hitch, but you might want to be thinking about another name. Her birth certificate says Tuesday Smith. No middle name. It doesn't do much for me, but you'll be the one to decide. At least Cheryl gave her your last name."

They talked for a few more minutes before Corporal Timothy Burrus Smith had to leave. "Look, they're calling for me, but hey—I love you, Dad."

Jake swallowed the lump in his throat and said gruffly, "Me, too, boy. You take real good care of yourself, we'll hold down the fort here until you can take over."

"My son, the soldier," he murmured, his eyes filming over. Not too long ago, Jake mused, he'd been changing the boy's diapers and feeding him disgusting stuff like pureed spinach and squash, while Rosemary strung beach-glass beads for a Nags Head crafts shop.

Now Rosemary was gone and Timmy was headed to the Middle East with his unit, and Jake was about to start the whole routine again, this time for his granddaughter. He didn't know if that made him feel older or younger—maybe a little of both.

On his way up the beach a short while later, Jake made three stops; two to check out problematic systems and one to pick up a large coffee and a cheese, turkey and apple sandwich. Next he called Sasha, only to be told everything was just fine, and she was getting ready to put the baby down for a nap. "While she's sleeping, I'll catch up on a few things, but you do know how often she eats, don't you? Every three hours. Are you sure you're ready for that?"

He wasn't sure of anything at this point.

Well, for one thing, he was hungry. He could eat while he was on stakeout, not that he expected to catch the guy in action.

Renters had already arrived at the cottage where he

usually took up a position. Three cars filled the parking area, one carrying a kayak on top, two others with surfboard racks. Jake cruised slowly along the narrow blacktop, looking for an unobtrusive place to park.

"Well, hell," he muttered, spotting a car pulled up beside Driftwinds. He recognized it as belonging to the rental agent only because he'd had Hack run her plates the first day Jake had staked out the place. He'd seen her around, an attractive brunette, probably under thirty. "Lady, you're in my way," he muttered, wondering whether to wait for her to leave or to give up now.

On the other hand, if he was waiting for the coast to clear, maybe Jamison was waiting, too. Odds were about one in ten thousand, but what the devil, until Hack could come up with another lead—and as long as he was here with a sandwich and a cup of coffee that was growing cold—he might as well stick around a few more minutes. The agent was probably checking to make sure Sasha had finished the job. That shouldn't take long.

He bit into his sandwich as he crept along the street in search of an out-of-the-way parking place, thinking about all that had happened since he'd shot a bunch of pictures of a luscious redhead only a few days ago, under the illusion that she was Jamison's girlfriend. The setting sun had turned her hair to flame while a light breeze had blown her flimsy blouse against her breasts. And those crazy pink shoes, he thought, grinning at the memory.

Oh, hell. Those shoes....

The one he'd taken off her foot was still on his dresser. Thank God the painters had finished his bedroom first; he'd hate to get the reputation of having a foot fetish.

Spotting an empty driveway near the end of the cul-de-sac where he would have a clear view of the Jamison place, he backed in and shut off the engine. His chances of catching Custer at his last stand were about the same as his chance of winning the lottery, but it wouldn't hurt to hang around for a few more minutes while he waited for Hack to come up with another lead.

According to the facts on file, the Jamisons had a small place in Colington over on the soundside, but with neighbors on either side, he would hardly show up there with another woman.

Jake flipped down the visor to cut the sun's glare. He'd just finished his sandwich and reached for his cell phone when he saw the rental agent come outside and head toward her car. "Okay, maybe now we'll see some action," he murmured, waiting for her to get in and drive off. Chances were slim to nothing, but he needed to be doing something, and until he got another lead, this was it.

He finished his coffee and was about to punch in the quick-dial number for the office when a familiar-looking guy in Bermuda shorts and yellow T-shirt emerged from the cottage, glanced around, and hurried across the gritty pavement toward the agent's car.

Jake's memory was good, but not perfect. He'd definitely seen the guy somewhere recently…but where? From one end of the Outer Banks to the other and occasionally into lower Virginia, he covered a lot of territory.

Where was this guy's car? And what had he been doing inside the cottage? Looking the place over with an eye to booking it later in the season?

The attractive brunette was still standing beside her car when yellow-shirt joined her there. They talked for a few minutes while Jake slouched in his seat and watched through a pair of aviator sunglasses, wishing he could read lips. About half his mind was on what he was seeing, the other half on the woman he'd left sleeping a few hours ago.

He shifted uncomfortably as his body reacted to the memory. The crazy thing was that if anyone had asked him to describe his ideal woman, Sasha Lasiter wouldn't have come to mind. So why was it that after only a few days he couldn't stop thinking about her?

More to the point, why did his body react with outrageous desire toward her? Hell, he was a grandfather, not some horny kid. He had a granddaughter to think about now, not to mention a job that at the moment was stalled in its tracks. So how come he was wasting time on a stakeout that obviously wasn't going to lead anywhere, thinking about a woman who had nothing at all to do with the case he was working, other than peripherally?

But instead of clearing his mind, he kept picturing the way she tried to stare him down with her multicolored eyes. Talk about attitude, she was a regular Ms. Napoleon. And the way she bragged about all her artifices—and the way she dressed....

It didn't take any special training to know that when people went to such lengths to disguise themselves there was usually a reason for it. The trouble was, he didn't know her well enough to figure it out. He knew she was sexier than any woman he'd ever met, and that included his late wife. He knew she was flat-out gorgeous, with or without her disguise. He'd seen her with her makeup smeared and with her face scrubbed clean of all but her freckles, and it hadn't made a speck of difference. She was who she was, and it was who she was that attracted him in a way that no other woman ever had.

Jake reminded himself again that she'd had four husbands and not a one of them had suited her well enough to keep. He'd had one wife, who had suited him very well during the few years they'd been together.

Bottom line—what could a glamorous, successful woman possibly see in a dull, middle-aged businessman, a mediocre detective who couldn't even manage a simple surveillance, who didn't know a damn thing about interior decoration, much less care about it—who didn't think one way or another about fashion as long as what he had on was comfortable?

Answer? Not a whole lot.

What did he see in her? A lot more than met the eye. That was the problem. Those colored contacts did a good job of disguising the shadows, but he'd heard that wistful note in her voice when she forgot to be Sasha the Outrageous. Somewhere under all that paint and polish there was a real woman who made him want to explore more than her body.

That is, if he ever got tired of exploring her body.

"What the hell?" he muttered suddenly. Sitting up, he removed his sunglasses in time to see yellow-shirt and the agent come together in a clinch that sent heat weaves shimmering off the tarmac.

"Well, now…" he mused, stroking his jaw. Maybe he wasn't such a lousy P.I., after all. His brain might not be up to speed, but evidently his instincts were still on the job. Jamison looked older than his campaign posters, but there was no mistaking that face.

Time to find out more about the attractive brunette

who, unless he was mistaken, worked for Southern Dunes Property Management. And who better to tell him than the decorator who'd been commissioned to update one of her rentals?

"Don't be so stingy, Faylene, let me hold her," Marty reached for the baby only to have Faylene turn away with her.

"You got you a husband now. Go home and make one o' your own, this one belongs to me and Sasha, don't you, sugar dumplin'?" The housekeeper beamed at the infant in her arms. "Lawhepus, if I weren't too old, I'd have me one of these in a minute."

"That'd be one for the records," Sasha observed dryly. "Last I heard it took nine months." Her feet were propped on a cushion on the coffee table that was littered with sample books and baby paraphernalia. She had managed to squeeze in a shower between feeding and bathing the baby before her friends had showed up, but she'd spent more time rocking Peaches and trying to remember the words to the song about the looking glass and the mockingbird.

With those dark blue eyes gazing up at her so solemnly, she had choked up more than once. Watching now as her friends exclaimed over her, Sasha told herself that what she was feeling was protectiveness, not possessiveness. A few more minutes and she would put an end to it. Too much stimulation wasn't good for an infant who wasn't yet two months old.

"Did I tell you I've got us another bachelor? Kell has this carpenter friend—actually, he's more of a contractor. He's recently divorced, no kids, no noticeably bad habits." Marty leaned over the housekeeper to cup a tiny foot in her hand.

"What does he look like? Anyone a tall, gorgeous blonde with a degree in accounting might be interested in?" Sasha continued to buff her short, newly exposed fingernails. She felt naked without the acrylic versions, but long nails and babies didn't go together.

Faylene glanced up. "I thought we'd already picked out this security fellow for Lily."

"Jake has other priorities now," Sasha reminded her friends.

"So?" Marty gave up trying to steal the infant away from the housekeeper and began leafing through a catalog of accessories.

"So he has enough on his mind without getting involved in a new relationship. Besides, his son's headed overseas and Jake's in the middle of repainting his house and, like I said, now he's got this baby to think about."

"Well, pardon me, but it looks like Jake's baby has all the caregivers she needs. So why can't he take a few hours off and go to our darned fund-raiser?" Marty shot her a pointed look. "Unless you have other plans for him?"

"Don't be silly!" Sasha snapped. Feeling her face grow warm, she said, "I hardly even know the man."

Faylene glanced up from the baby on her lap. "I told you about them letters Lily's been getting, didn't I? The ones with the numbers on the front like a secret code or something? I asked her about it the other day when I saw her looking all weepy-eyed over one. She's been getting 'em, one a week, for as long as I've been working for her."

"Faye, for heaven's sake, you know better than to

gossip about things like that," Marty scolded. "What'd she say?"

"Pretended like she didn't hear me."

"It's probably a service person—someone in the military."

"I 'spect so," murmured the older woman, her attention on the infant gazing up at her so intently. "Did I tell you they're written in pencil on lined paper? First I thought it was a street number on front, but that was on the next line. A San Pedro Street—something like that."

"There's nothing like that around here," Sasha said thoughtfully. "Florida? Maybe St. Augustine?"

"Nope, California."

"Well, whatever it is, it's none of our business," Marty said self-righteously, and then spoiled the effect by suggesting it might be a tax number. "She is a CPA, after all. Maybe you misread the CA for CPA." Faylene's reading skills were on a par with her cooking.

"Not that it matters, but if you're that curious, ask her about it," Sasha said, closing the matter.

"Back to the fund-raiser, you don't mind missing it, do you, Sash? You can baby-sit for a few hours while we get your guy together with Lily, can't you?"

Sasha had an idea her friend was playing with her. She buffed harder. Before she could come up with a reason to take Jake out of the race, she heard a car pull up out in front.

Marty peered through the window. "Speak of the devil," she said, a wide grin spreading over her face.

Ten

Jake came to a full stop just inside the doorway. The expression on his face was priceless. Amused, Sasha watched his reaction to finding himself outnumbered by females.

Faylene looked up and broke into a broad smile, rearranging scores of wrinkles on her heavily made-up face. "Hey there. I gotcha baby here. She don't look much like you, I'll say that for her."

Marty said, "Well, hi there."

"Uh…ladies," he murmured cautiously.

Sasha said, "Now I know what Daniel must have looked like standing in the door of the lion's den. Come on in, Jake, we were just talking about you. You've met my friends, haven't you?"

He nodded and then his gaze returned to the baby in Faylene's lap. Waving tiny pink fists, Tuesday Smith, aka

Peaches, was making noises that Sasha recognized as meaning, "Enough with this hands-on stuff, I need a nap."

Evidently, Jake had forgotten how to interpret baby language. "Is she—?"

"Hurting? Don't think so. Starving? No way, she was fed less than half an hour ago. Wet? Probably. Mostly, she's just ready for a nap, aren't you, sugar? We're still working on a mutually convenient schedule."

Sasha scooped the baby from Faylene's lap and moved closer so that Jake could see her tiny face. Inhaling the warm soap-and-outdoorsy scent of his skin, she told herself with a sense of mystic certainty that blindfolded, and with nothing more than that, she could have picked him out of any lineup. It had to be pheromones, she thought wistfully. She couldn't afford for it to be anything more complicated than chemistry. Even that was almost more than she could handle. "Thank you for sending my car home," she murmured.

Jake nodded. "No problem."

While he concentrated on the baby, Sasha happened to glance at Marty, who was looking him over with undisguised interest.

The bookseller caught her eye, winked and blushed. "We were just talking about the fund-raiser planned for tomorrow night, Jake. Did Sasha tell you about it?"

"What fund-raiser?"

"It's just a local project," Sasha dismissed. "I doubt if you'd be interested." Turning away, she sank down onto the sofa and lifted the baby to her shoulder, patting her on the back.

As the two most comfortable chairs were taken, Jake settled beside her, his weight tilting the cushion so that she found herself leaning on his shoulder. "What kind of local project?" he asked.

Their voices overlapping, Marty and Faylene described the summer camp that featured fishing, kayaking, camping and even fly-tying. "It costs two hundred bucks for a two-week session," said Marty.

"I got a good friend, Bob Ed Cutrell, down at the marina," Faylene said. "You might know him—he outfits 'em so the gear don't cost nothing extra, but—"

Marty picked up. "But a lot of them still can't afford it. This is not exactly a high-income district, in case you hadn't noticed. Commercial fishing barely makes expenses these days, and the storm flooded so many fields, it'll take at least another year to recover."

To Sasha, seated beside him on the sofa, it seemed the most natural thing in the world to lean against Jake Smith while holding his baby in her arms. Gazing down at the small bundle sleeping so peacefully on her shoulder, she murmured, "What about it, sweety pie, you want to go to summer camp?"

Marty looked from Sasha to Jake, as if trying to measure the degree of involvement. "So what about it, Jake—shall we count you in?"

If Jake felt pressured, he was tactful enough not to show it. "Can I get back to you?" When he reached for the infant, his hands brushed against Sasha's breast. "Here you go, baby, come to Granddad."

As if his touch weren't enough to melt any residual resistance she might feel, his voice finished her off. Fighting against the urge to trade places with the baby in his arms, Sasha tugged the pink flannel square from her shoulder and spread it over his.

"I'd forgotten about that part," Jake said, obviously not really bothered by the risk of a damp shoulder. They traded lingering smiles until the other two women stood and collected their purses.

"Guess we'd better be going," said Marty, a gleam of amusement in her eyes. "I brought you a few more books. Since you're temporarily house-bound, you might even get caught up on your reading." She indicated the stack of paperbacks on the floor beside the cluttered escritoire.

Faylene said, "I turned the fridge back on after I wiped it out, so don't open the door till it has a chance to catch up."

"Don't bother to see us out," Marty said dryly as the two women exchanged unmistakable smirks.

"Did I miss something?" Jake asked when the front door closed behind them.

"I hope so. They mean well, but—" Sasha shook her head. She wasn't about to tell him about the matchmaking she and her friends occasionally did—especially after the way Marty had looked at the two of them together, as if measuring them for a double harness.

"Here, I'll take her now—she's yawning."

How could any man be so darned tempting with a baby in his arms, spit-up on his shirt and a goofy grin on his face? All she had to do was look at him to remember last night and what had probably been the biggest mistake of her life.

Which, considering her track record, was saying a lot.

"Give me another few minutes. Look, the reason I came by—we need to talk."

Uh-oh. Crunch time. She'd known it was coming, she

just hadn't wanted to think about it. Once he took the baby home with him, he'd have no reason to return to Muddy Landing.

Feeling as if she were dragging an anchor, she stood and reached for the baby to take her upstairs. Jake sighed and reluctantly handed her over.

When she came downstairs a few minutes later, he said, "Without breaking any confidences, what can you tell me about the agent handling the Jamison rental?"

"Katie McIver?" Puzzled, Sasha wondered what the rental agent had to do with their baby. "I've known her several years, but only in a business capacity. I did their offices—Southern Dunes Property Management? Since then she's called me several times for makeovers and quick patch-up jobs. Mostly the owners take care of that sort of thing themselves, but now and then they leave it to the agency." She settled down, this time in the armchair instead of the sofa. "I know she's well respected. I know she handles several of their top rentals. Other than that, I don't really know much about her."

Jake nodded silently, as if he were processing the information. "Do you know if she's married?"

"We've never really discussed much besides budgets and timetables. Once we had coffee together at Southern Bean, but I don't remember anything we talked about except the damage Hurricane Isabel did to her cottages." Increasingly puzzled, she asked, "Why do you need to know all this?"

Absently, Jake stroked his jaw. "Then you wouldn't happen to know if she's, um—involved in a relationship?"

"I told you, we've never discussed anything like that. Is there a reason why you need to know?" She forced herself to stamp down a twinge of jealousy. Katie had to be on the sunny side of thirty. She'd probably end up managing the agency one of these days, because she was every bit as smart as she was attractive. "Why don't you just ask her? I don't like talking about people behind their back."

The vertical lines between his dark eyebrows deepened. "Sorry. I shouldn't have asked. Something unexpected came up on my way here and I wanted to get a feel for it before I went any further."

"I read enough suspense novels to know about questioning witnesses. I couldn't help you even if I wanted to. Why don't you ask Katie whatever it is you want to know? I've got her cell phone number if I can remember where I put it."

"This case I was working on when you and I met?"

"When you invaded my privacy, you mean," she corrected. Arms crossed over her bosom, she tried a chilly look, but she was in too deep. She gave up trying. "But then you came to my rescue after I hurt my ankle, so I suppose we're even," she admitted grudgingly.

"Yeah, well…things got sort of crazy there for a while. I don't know how much I told you before, but the owners of the cottage where you were, ah—"

"Working, but taking a tiny, well-earned break," she supplied before he could accuse her of goofing off on the job.

"Right. Anyway, they're getting a divorce and the wife hired me to check out her suspicions concerning her husband and another woman. She got the idea he was using their cottage as a—a—"

"Love nest?" Sasha thought about the scent of cigarette smoke and the rumpled cushions. And there was the cork she'd found in an otherwise empty trash can.

"I don't know how much love was involved, but yeah—I guess you could call it that."

"Did she have any evidence? The wife, I mean?"

"A friend told her she'd heard rumors that Jamison might be using the place as his private playground." Jake settled into the green leather-covered chair. "Evidence is what I'm supposed to get."

Indignation built swiftly. "You took all those pictures of me thinking I was waiting to meet a lover? I don't know whether to be amused, flattered or insulted." She settled on amusement as the least problematic.

"Hey, I never claimed to be one of those super sleuths you read about or watch on TV. Every now and then I like to try my hand at something besides security systems just to prove I'm not—"

"Over the hill," she finished for him, and stopped just short of saying, take it from me, you're not.

Judging from his expression, the same thought occurred to Jake. Sasha settled on the sofa, putting the coffee table between them.

Over the hill?

Uh-uh, no way. She'd had lovers both older and younger. Jake was in a class by himself.

He smiled. "I was going to say rusty, but back to what we were talking about." The smile faded. "My client called a few days ago to say they'd gotten back together and my services were no longer needed. She called again just as I was about to leave this morning."

"To say what, sic him?"

Jake nodded. "Words to that effect."

"And—?" Sasha prompted.

"And I just came across evidence possibly involving your rental agent."

"What evidence? Circumstantial? Gossip?"

"Nothing circumstantial about a lip-lock that timed out at just under two minutes."

"You're kidding," she said slowly. "Katie and Mr. Jamison? How can you be sure? I've never even seen the man, much less met him. I've never met either of the owners."

"His face is plastered on campaign posters every time we have another election. One of the reasons why he can't just book a room for a few hours." Jake described the frustrating, off-again, on-again case he'd been working on for the past several days.

"Hmm…you know what it sounds like to me?" Rising, Sasha went to the bottom of the stairs and listened for sounds from the baby. A moment later, she settled back into the chair. "All's quiet. Bless her heart, she'll probably sleep for another hour, at least." Taking a deep breath, she said, "You know what I think? I think he patched things up just long enough to throw his wife off guard and get her signature on a few documents." The soft contours of her face hardened imperceptibly. "Any woman who signs anything at all under those circumstances—anything but a restraining order—is asking for trouble."

When he continued to watch her, she averted her face. "Have you ever had to sign one of those?" He sounded grim.

"We're not talking about me. Besides, the kind of man who needs a restraining order usually ignores it."

"Sasha?"

He waited.

Finally, she said, "One of my husbands was…physical. When he drank too much, or when I didn't do things just fast enough or high enough to suit him."

Jake closed his eyes momentarily, as if ignoring it could change the past.

She shrugged. "At least by the time I was old enough to marry, I'd learned how to handle—that sort of thing. I only had to get a restraining order once."

Jake leaned forward as if to rise, but she shook her head. "Honey, let me tell you something, if shedding husbands was an Olympic sport, I'd win gold every single time." She laughed, but with her eyes glittering, the effect was hardly amusing. "You want me to advise your client on the proper way to get rid of unwanted rodents?"

He couldn't think of a single thing to say—nothing that made sense under the circumstances. He'd known her for less than a week, yet he'd instinctively trusted her with his granddaughter. He'd seen her all dressed up in her fancy outfits, her makeup and her gaudy jewelry—he'd seen her barefoot, wearing a shapeless, colorless tent with her makeup smeared over half her face.

Either way, the effect she had on him was the same. The thought of any man mistreating her made his blood boil. She might pretend to be tough, but it didn't take a security expert to see through her defenses.

With a Sashalike toss of the head, she said, "Peaches is probably going to sleep for a while, so why don't I make us something for lunch? Or have you already eaten?"

* * *

Over Marty's leftover casserole Sasha asked about the progress on his house. She had tiptoed upstairs to check on the sleeping baby.

Jake said, "Another few days and the work will be finished. I can use a window fan to pump the place out." He asked about any commitments she had that might take her out of town over the next several days, and she told him that wouldn't be a problem.

"This close to the season, I've already done most of the hands-on work." She wouldn't allow it to be a problem. She happened to be in the middle of doing a new suite of offices and was angling to get a bid on another one, but Marty or Faye could baby-sit if she had to run over to the beach. At least she had her car back now, even if her ankle wasn't quite a hundred percent.

Sasha watched his throat move as he finished off his iced tea. In all her experience with the opposite sex it had never even occurred to her that the throat was a major erogenous zone.

On the other hand, just thinking about the way he had flicked his tongue in the hollow at the base of her throat was enough to steal the air right out of her lungs.

Jake caught her staring and lifted one eyebrow. He looked delicious, but then, when had he ever looked any other way? The man was no clotheshorse, which suited her just fine, having been married to a couple of *GQ* types.

"About Katie and Jamison—are you sure?" she asked. "Maybe it was just an air kiss. I mean, if she's been managing his cottage all these years, chances are they're friends."

"You want a demonstration?" Shoving his chair back from the table, Jake took her hand and pulled her to her feet. "They were standing about like this."

He was no more than five inches away, close enough to feel the heat, to smell his soap and after-shave. Sasha breathed deeply, as if to fill herself with his essence. Her pulse was pounding, her lips parted and waited.

"She was facing me—his back was to me, but once he moved closer, like this—" Jake closed the distance until her breasts were pressed against his chest "—I couldn't see all that much, but I seriously doubt if they were discussing the weather." His voice was starting to sound thick, almost strangled.

Sasha couldn't have spoken if her life depended on it.

"Actually, I think it was more like this," he whispered, his breath stirring tendrils of hair against her face.

Just as it had before, his kiss began slowly with a soft, moist touch—a gentle, teasing brush of lips that quickly escalated into a major event. Was there a Richter scale for kisses?

If so, his registered at least a twelve.

Standing on her tiptoes, Sasha lifted her arms around his neck and pressed against him. Through two layers of clothing, she couldn't get close enough. While his teasing tongue explored her mouth, driving her mad with need, his hands cupped her hips, moving her back and forth against his erection until her trembling legs were barely able to support her. She could feel the moisture gathering, preparing her for what was to come.

Lifting his mouth from hers, he whispered, "Is that bed still available?"

His hands cupped her breasts, his thumbs stroking her taut nipples. She managed to nod. At this point, speech was beyond her. This is crazy, she thought. She was already in over her head. If he took her to bed one more time, she might sink without a trace.

Exactly what are your intentions, Mr. Smith?

Great sex, what else?

Exactly! Great sex and what else?

But if ever there was a time for that old T-shirt philosophy to kick in, it was now. She shut up and went with the flow.

Jake closed the bedroom door and turned to her, his eyes glittering with an intensity that was purely electric. "You're sure?"

Reading her answer in her eyes—there were some things no amount of artifice could hide—he pulled off his shirt and unbuckled his belt. Then, with his jeans unfastened, they came together for another bone-melting kiss, and any lingering uncertainty she might have harbored about the way she felt melted right along with her bones.

Using both hands, she slid his jeans and briefs down over his hips, then laughed shakily when he nearly stumbled trying to kick them off over his shoes.

"Oh, no," he taunted, "you're not getting me naked while you're still wrapped up in that circus tent. I know all about power plays."

"This circus tent, as you call it, just happens to be the most comfortable thing I own," she informed him, her voice muffled as she pulled the caftan over her head. At least it was one of her newer ones. Besides, it was a little late to dash upstairs and change into something from Victoria's Secret.

The moment she was undressed, Jake lowered her to the bed and came down beside her. "You're incredibly beautiful," he murmured.

She was so far gone she actually believed him. "So are you," she whispered. "Your nose—"

"Broken twice."

"Your eyes…"

"Reading glasses."

"Me, too," she admitted, but then all thought of minor flaws disappeared. When she trailed her fingers through the narrow pelt of flat curls that arrowed down from his chest, past his hard middle to his groin, Jake sucked his breath audibly.

He was hard *everywhere.*

He kissed her eyes, her nose, and then he found her mouth again, hurling her into another dimension. The only reality was the aching, pulsating sweetness that left her helpless and needy, from the top of her Spice Tea hair to her Rhinestone Pink toenails. She shivered as his hands skimmed down her sides to cup her hips. When his fingers spanned the exquisitely sensitive skin of her groin, tracing the line and teasing her with quick forays into her moist center, her hips moved involuntarily.

She gasped, "Please—I need—"

"Hold on while I—"

"Now," she begged.

"First I need to—"

She could feel him hot and hard and heavy, pulsing against her. When he leaned on one elbow to reach the bedside table, she knew what he was doing. She'd seen him remove the foil package from his wallet and place it there. By her own standards, at least, she'd been safe and sensible all her life, and look where it had got her.

He covered her hand with his and began moving it toward ground zero. When her hand closed around him she forgot to breathe.

He groaned. Moving against her palm, he whispered, "No—no, wait a minute—"

As if waiting were even a faint possibility. He was like molten steel, and she wanted him desperately, wildly, far beyond the reach of common sense. She wanted him any way she could have him, but most of all she wanted him inside her where a five-alarm need was blazing out of control.

Using her thumb to caress, she squeezed and stroked, slowly at first and then faster. Curled around his naked back, her hips moved in unison with her hand until he gripped her wrist, lifting her hand away.

Moments later he moved over her again. "Now," he whispered roughly as he plunged inside her hot, tight center. The sweetest pleasure pulsated around them as they raced toward the finish line. All too soon her climax triggered his and Jake shouted hoarsely, collapsing on top of her.

Eventually, with both their bodies slick with sweat, he rolled onto his back, pulling her on top of him. Later, when she could gather enough energy to speak, Sasha said, "I'm too heavy for you."

He barely opened his eyes. "You move and I'll…"

"Take your toys and go home?" she teased lazily.

"Yeah, something like that." He grinned without opening his eyes. A few minutes later, when both their pulse rates slowed to something approximating normal, he said, "What toys are we talking about, hmm?"

She chuckled. "The one I'm playing with at the moment?"

There went the old pulse rate again, like one of those test-your-strength gizmos at the county fair. "It takes two to play that game."

"I know," she purred. "Interested in a rematch?"

"You talked me into it."

"Best two out of three?"

"You're on," he drawled, and rolled over onto his side, facing her.

This time they made love at almost a leisurely pace. Sated, they took the time to explore, to discover and exploit newly sensitized areas that had been neglected in their earlier rush.

One tiny spot between her thigh and her belly. Attention there drove her wild.

The thin skin behind Jake's knees and the arches of his feet, where a single stroke could render him helpless. Sasha tickled him there, then took advantage of his helplessness to kiss every inch of his torso, lingering in places that made him close his eyes and groan. When it was her turn, he returned the favor. She twisted and whimpered under his sweet assault until neither of them could wait another second.

This time she straddled him, clasping him with her thighs. Panting, she matched him stroke for stroke, her head flung back, her eyes tightly closed. She felt herself tightening around him, heard him cry out her name, and then she collapsed, her sweat-damp body melting into his.

Eventually, Jake said, "That's it. Write me off as a casualty."

Sliding off him onto her side, Sasha curled up in a fetal position—as if that might postpone facing reality. Either she'd forgotten everything she'd ever known about men—about sex—or she'd just entered an alternate reality.

She thought, I hardly even know this man, but I don't know if I can live without him. Oh, God, what have I done?

I'm not ready for this, Jake thought. He pretended to be asleep because he wasn't ready to answer any questions. In case she asked any questions.

In case she asked what? About his intentions?

Who had "intentions" in these days of instant gratification? You parked your brain, unleashed your libido, a good time was had by all, and that was the end of it, right?

Wrong. He knew better than that. He'd always known better than that, even in his wildest oat-sowing days. The trouble was, this woman had somehow managed to infiltrate his dull, orderly life until now she was as necessary to him as the air he breathed. He had no idea how it had happened, he only knew it had.

While she'd been watching him undress, he'd been thanking his lucky stars he'd been a swimmer all his life. He could still run five miles, although not with any great speed. There might be a few gray hairs on his head, but the hair on his body was still dark.

She stirred beside him and murmured, "Jake?"

"Hmm?" A smart man would get up, get dressed and get going before he got in any deeper. But then, he'd never been known for his intellect.

"You 'wake?"

"Umm-hmm."

When she rolled over toward him, his hand brushed against her. The gentle swell of her belly was far sexier than anything revealed by all those rail-thin, near-naked beach bunnies that flocked to the area each season. If ever a woman was made for love...

"Who won?" she murmured. He could tell by the sound of her voice that she was smiling.

So he smiled, too. "Who's keeping score? Call it a draw."

When they heard a familiar wail, he sat up. "I'll get her, honey, you stay here."

Still without opening her eyes, Sasha smiled. "You don't have to do that."

"You change her while I get a bottle ready."

Recovering from a state of boneless lethargy, Sasha managed to sit up just as Jake scooped up his clothes and disappeared into the bathroom, his pale buttocks in stark contrast to his lightly tanned thighs and darkly tanned back. Shoving her hair from her face, she glanced around for her clothes, pulled on the minimum and hurried upstairs.

By the time she reached the bedroom, it had occurred to her that a little later on, the guestroom might make a fine nursery. She could clear out the flea market and estate-sale finds she'd been storing there, maybe roll on a water-based paint—something in pink, with a border of Disney characters dancing across the top....

Just outside the door she stopped and closed her eyes. You idiot! Won't you ever learn? Never invest what you

can't afford to lose. Her second husband, who hadn't
bothered to practice what he preached, had taught her that.

Obviously, the lesson had been wasted.

Eleven

Jake left while Sasha was giving the baby a bottle. Fled the scene might be a better description. He felt like a deserter, but there was no way he was going to be able to get his mind back on track while she was tipped back in the big leather armchair, her bare feet on the coffee table, with his tiny granddaughter cradled in her arms. How any woman could manage to look sexy and maternal at the same time was a mystery to him. One he couldn't afford to dwell on, not when a single whiff of her hand lotion and he was rarin' to ride again.

He'd tried telling himself it was only sex, but there was no "only" about it. Nothing about Sasha Lasiter could ever be called "only." That's what made it so damn scary. He had known—all right, he had sensed—that there was something special about her right from the first. Why else would he have been snapping pictures of her even though they were evidence of nothing except that here was a beautiful woman.

And now things had gone too far to turn back, even if he'd wanted to turn back.

But before he could deal with any new beginnings, he had some old business to finish.

Hearing him drive off, Sasha felt like throwing something at him. "See you later," he'd called out as soon as she'd settled down with the baby. The coward!

Oh, he'd be back, she wasn't worried about that, but for what? Her or his baby? And what about after he took his baby home to his drab white-on-white house? What then? Would she ever see him again?

Setting the bottle on the coffee table, she eased the baby onto her shoulder. "Well, you've gone and done it now, haven't you, Sally June?"

Talk about jumping out of the frying pan into the fire.

Jake wasn't like all the others. That didn't mean he was perfect, it just meant that she had a whole new set of rules to learn. Unfortunately, despite all her experience, she'd jumped headfirst into the game without knowing where the boundaries were, what the stakes were.

No point in blaming it on Fate—not unless Fate had a terrific sense of humor. If anything, she'd have to blame it on a pink, spike-heeled, ankle-strap shoe. That's what had started it all.

She sighed, inhaling the sweet baby smell, taking comfort from the tiny warm bundle that fit so perfectly in the curve of her bosom. As much as she wanted his baby, she wanted the man even more. It was more than sex, although that had been unbelievably good. The chemistry between them was...explosive was the only word she could think of to describe it.

But it was far more than that. Right from the beginning there'd been something about the man that had fit into a hollow she didn't even know she possessed. Like two halves of a whole. Like two lovers reunited after lifetimes of being apart.

"Heaven help me," she whispered as she headed upstairs with the sleeping infant, "I've gone and done it again—fallen in love."

The next time the phone rang she was rinsing out a few tiny garments. Wiping her hands on her skirt, she grabbed the receiver. "Lasiter residence."

"How come you're answering like that?" Marty asked.

"Oh, hi. Because if it's a client, I'm not in, not until I can work out a baby-sitting schedule. Are you calling to sign up for a time slot?"

"Dream on. I've got my own business to run, remember?"

Sasha sighed. "I know that, I was only joking."

"Tired of playing mama so soon?"

"No way, but I've got an appointment at the beach tomorrow at three that I'd really like to keep. It shouldn't take but a couple of hours. How about it, can you spare Faylene that long? Tomorrow's your day, isn't it?"

"With Kell building our new addition on to the back and customers in and out the front, cleaning's hardly worth the effort, anyway, so Faye's free. Speaking of big events, did you get Jake lined up for Monday? I called earlier, but I guess you were out."

"Sorry, it didn't come up again after y'all left."

There was a long silence, and then Marty said softly, "Aw, honey.... You want him for yourself, don't you?"

Avoiding a direct answer, Sasha said, "You know what? I don't think Lily's all that interested in meeting anyone new. You know those letters Faye says she gets every week? Maybe she's already involved."

"And maybe they're from her maiden aunt. Anyway, it won't hurt to expose her to a few candidates."

"Go ahead and expose all you want to, just—"

Marty, whose intuition had a way of clicking on just when it was most inconvenient, finished the sentence. "Just not your guy, huh? Gotcha, hon. But at this rate we might as well give up matchmaking. We're running out of bachelors."

"There's still Gus and Egbert."

"You jest. Lily and Gus don't even speak the same language, and she's taller and smarter than Egbert."

"Well, what about that guy at the license bureau, the one with the dimples? I heard he's single."

"Ever seen him out from behind that desk? Major spare tire."

"So? Bob Ed's spare tire doesn't seem to bother Faylene," Sasha reminded her friend.

"Look, Kell's calling—I gotta go, but you just concentrate on reeling Jake in, y'hear? This time you've got yourself a keeper."

"I have?" Sasha murmured softly after replacing the

phone. Then why did she feel like she'd just jumped off a high building without so much as an umbrella to slow the fall?

To say Jake was frustrated was an understatement. Sasha's landline was busy, she wasn't answering her cell phone; he had those two installations to do before the weekend, and he finally had a solid lead in the Jamison case. Now all he had to do was prove it.

The trouble was, he couldn't seem to focus on anything but racing back to Muddy Landing. Back to Sasha and his grandbaby.

Probably a good thing he couldn't reach her by phone. If he told her he was on the way and she said not to bother, then what? When it came to this crazy business of falling in love, he was years out of practice. Some things got easier the second time around. Some things didn't.

In the meantime, he had a job to do. Pulling in at Southern Dunes Property Management, he looked around for a white Durango with a personalized license plate. Now that most rentals, including Driftwinds, were booked solid for the season, Jamison and his playmate would have to make other arrangements. Rather than risk his vehicle being spotted where he had no business being, a smart man would park elsewhere and hitch a ride with someone else.

In this case, his lover—who might have a legitimate reason for parking outside an empty cottage.

McIver's car was missing from her designated parking place. He spotted Jamison's Durango half hidden by a giant oleander bush. Unless the gentleman was inside the office, three guesses where he could be found.

Make that with whom he could be found. Jake didn't have to catch them in bed together; all he had to do was catch the two of them together in a place where Jamison had no business being. A smart lawyer should be able to use circumstantial evidence and a guilty conscience as leverage.

When he walked inside he was carrying a conspicuous envelope that happened to contain his truck registration and maintenance record. The reception area was empty except for a middle-aged woman behind a small desk.

"May I help you, sir?"

"I'm looking for Katie—Katie McIver?"

"I'm sorry, you just missed her." She looked at the envelope. "If you'd like to leave that here, I could give it to her when she comes in."

"You wouldn't know where I could find her, would you? I won't take up but a minute of her time, but it's important."

It was midafternoon when Sasha heard the slam of a car door out in the driveway. Her heart skipped a beat and began to pound as she glanced through the window. She was furious with Jake for staying away so long. He could have called to see how Peaches was doing, if nothing else.

She touched her hair. Determined not to take extra pains, she'd shoved it up and anchored it with a clip, trusting nature and gravity to do the rest. Wearing layered tank tops in pink and orange and a sheer flow-

ered skirt—casual, but flattering—she took her time
going down the stairs. No shoes, but a toe ring on each
foot.

By the time he rang the doorbell, she was cool and
composed. As for the flush on her face, she had no control over that. Taking a deep, steadying breath, she arranged a polite smile. "Well, hi, Jake."

Polite. Friendly. Palpitations don't count.

"I thought I'd stop by to see if you needed anything,"
he said.

She stepped back, affecting an offhand manner.
"Since you just happened to be in the neighborhood?"

They both knew he had no real business in Muddy
Landing. He'd already admitted as much. "Should I
have made an appointment?"

Sasha shook her head. Maybe she needed a dose of
that allergy medication they advertised so much. Not
only palpitations, but hoarseness and watery eyes. "You
want to see her?" she asked when she could trust her voice
not to give her away. "She's upstairs. I just put her down.
She stayed awake a long time after her last bottle."

Jake cleared his throat. If she didn't know better
she'd think he was as self-conscious as she was. "I,
uh—could we talk first?"

Oh, God, he had something to say that she wasn't going
to like hearing. He was taking his baby and leaving for
good. "You know, she's much better off here. Changes
can't be good for her—she's already had too many."

"Yeah, I'm with you there." Jake swallowed hard.
She could see his throat working, see the tension in his
eyes. "Look, I'm about as far out in left field as I've ever

been in my life, but Sasha—have I been taking too much for granted? I mean, this is crazy, right? We've known each other less than a week."

Closing her eyes Sasha held her breath and uttered a silent prayer. This was not about the baby, this was about—

"Would you like to come in?" she asked.

Leading the way into the living room, she lowered herself carefully at one end of the sofa. Jake took the other end. Her face still felt hot. His was about as pale as someone with a perennial tan could be.

She waited for him to get to the point.

"Look, you don't have to take it if you don't like it. I mean, you've already got so many. Or we can exchange it. It might not even fit, I wasn't sure of what size you wore."

"You bought me a pair of *shoes?*"

Wordlessly, he shook his head. He turned toward her, one knee hitched up onto the cushion so that the other one was practically on the floor. A shaft of late-morning sunshine slanted through the window to highlight the salt-and-pepper gray at his temples.

He looked gorgeous and sexy and totally out of his depth.

Her heart kicked into overdrive. "Jake, what are you trying to say?" She didn't dare try to guess. If she guessed wrong, she'd be devastated.

He opened his left hand, and there on his palm was a small jeweler's box. "I'm doing this all wrong, aren't I? I should have said something first."

"Say something *now,*" she exclaimed.

"Hoo-boy, this is kind of hard to put into words, but

here it goes." He took a deep breath. "You know about me—about Rosemary, I mean. We were young, but I loved her with all my heart. There hasn't been any-one—not serious, I mean—since then."

His self-deprecating smile hurt her heart. She closed her eyes until he whispered, "Until now."

Only then did she dare allow herself to hope, having learned caution in a hard school.

"Sasha, ever since we got together, things have been screwed up. Normally, these things—I mean, you and me—well, it usually takes longer. You know what I mean."

Slowly, she shook her head. "I haven't a clue."

"Okay, let me say this. For the past dozen years or so since I lost Rosemary, I've managed pretty well. We'd just started the business, so I could concentrate on that, but mostly I concentrated on Timmy. He was too young to understand why his mother wasn't there, but as he got older, things got better. You lost a brother, so you know how it is. You don't forget, but after a while you move on. You know what I'm saying?"

She hadn't a clue. Yes, she knew what grief felt like. So did he. But that was years ago, and this was now. He was still clutching the ring box. She didn't even glance at it. Instead she stared him in the eye through her turquoise contacts. If he thought he could just pay her off for services rendered—baby-sitting and other-wise—with a piece of jewelry, she would kill him. Flat-out kill him!

His shoulders fell. He closed his eyes briefly and then said, "I think maybe I'm all alone out here, so how about knocking me in the head and calling Hack to come pick up the body."

"Jake, what is it you're trying to say?"

Ignoring her, he continued speaking, as if he had to get it all out before he ran out of breath. "But if you happen to feel anything like the same way I do, then maybe you could wear my ring and we could sort of explore this thing as we go along. Please?"

Oh, yes, oh, yes, oh, yes!

Some men were glib, others needed help. Sasha was nothing if not helpful. "Jake, if you're trying to ask if I want to have an—an affair, then—"

He shook his head. Her hopes took a sharp dip, then recovered.

"Or I guess we could start out that way if you want to. Sort of take things gradually, get to know each other better. Then maybe in a few days—that is, a few weeks…"

To heck with caution. She reached for his hand. Ignoring the ring box, she pulled him into her arms, knowing she was taking the chance of a lifetime. "I thought you'd never ask," she whispered.

A few hours later, barefoot and shirtless with his jeans unsnapped at the waist, Jake brought her coffee in bed. "Two sugars and a dash of diet cream, right?"

Sasha sat up and gave him a smug, lazy smile. "This is so decadent, but then I've always adored decadence." Other than her new ring, designed and made by a Nags Head goldsmith, of yellow gold and white, with three small diamonds, she wore only a sated look.

"Is it teachable?"

"What, decadence?" She held open the bedcovers, scented with sex and Odalisque and essence of Jake. "With me as your tutor, you'll master the art in no time."

"Hey, let's not be in too big a hurry," he said, his voice huskier than usual. "Let's give it a few decades, shall we?"

* * * * *

THE CRENSHAWS OF TEXAS

**Brothers bound by blood
and the land they call home!**

DOUBLE IDENTITY

(Silhouette Desire #1646,
available April 2005)

by Annette Broadrick

Undercover agent Jude Crenshaw
had only gotten involved with
Carina Patterson for the sake of
cracking a smuggling case against
her brothers. But close quarters soon
led to a shared attraction, and Jude
could only hope his double identity
wouldn't break both their hearts.

*Available at your
favorite retail outlet.*

Silhouette Desire

COMING NEXT MONTH

#1645 JUST A TASTE—Bronwyn Jameson
Dynasties: The Ashtons
When Jillian Ashton's arrogant husband died, it wasn't long before she
found a man who treated her right—*really* right. Problem was, Seth—
a tall, dark and handsome hunk—was her late husband's brother. She'd
planned on just a taste of his tender touch, but was left wanting more....

#1646 DOUBLE IDENTITY—Annette Broadrick
The Crenshaws of Texas
Undercover agent Jude Crenshaw only meant to attract Carina Patterson
for the sake of cracking a case against her brothers. But when close
quarters turned his business into their pleasure, Jude could only hope his
double identity wouldn't turn their new union into two broken hearts.

#1647 RULES OF ATTRACTION—Susan Crosby
Behind Closed Doors
P.I. Quinn Gerard was following a suspected accomplice—or so he
thought. When the sexy bombshell turned out to be her twin sister, Claire,
Quinn no longer had to watch her every move. But he couldn't seem to
take his eyes off her! Could Quinn convince Claire to bend the rules and
give in to their mutual attraction?

#1648 WHEN THE EARTH MOVES—Roxanne St. Claire
After Jo Ellen Tremaine's best friend died during an earthquake, she
was determined to adopt her friend's baby girl. But first she needed
the permission of the girl's stunningly sexy uncle—big-shot attorney
Cameron McGrath. Cameron always had a weakness for wildly attractive
women, but neither was prepared for the aftershocks of this seismic shift....

#1649 BEYOND BUSINESS—Rochelle Alers
The Blackstones of Virginia
Blackstone Farms owner Sheldon Blackstone couldn't help but be
enraptured by his newly hired assistant, Renee Williams. Little did he
know she was pregnant with her ex's baby. Renee was totally taken by
this older man, but could she convince him to make her—and her
child—his forever?

#1650 SLEEPING ARRANGEMENTS—Amy Jo Cousins
The terms of the will were clear: in order to gain her inheritance
Addy Tyler needed to be married. Enter the one man she never dreamed
would become her groom of convenience—Spencer Reed. Their marriage
was supposed to be hands-off, but their sleeping arrangements changed
everything!

SDCNM0305